CW00468185

Born To Royalty

Sarah Emambocus

Published by Sarah Emambocus, 2022.

BORN TO ROYALTY

First edition. June 15, 2022.

Copyright © 2022 Sarah Emambocus.

ISBN: 979-8201938086

Written by Sarah Emambocus.

Table of Contents

Chapter 1

Have you ever fallen in love with someone so much that you just wanna be with them for the rest of your life? The story begins with two young people, who fell in love. In the deep forest of Aetas, a young man is walking down a path holding a map as he thinks, *'I think I am heading in the right direction'* Suddenly, he stops as he is captivated by a mysterious person and wonders, *'whoa... who is she?'*. The young girl turns around as the guy keeps staring at her as she wonders, *'is he just going to stare at me or come over to speak?'*. The wind and sunlight blow lightly over the young girl as the guy comes over nervously and apologizes as she rolls her eyes. He asks, *"what's your name?"*. She laughs replying *"you get straight to the point, don't you?"*. He nods as she smiles saying, *"my name is Amelia; people call me Amy what's yours?"*. He nervously looks at her thinking *'I can't let her know my real name...'*. Amelia says, *"I hope you understand I know who you are, I was just being friendly"*. He looks at her stunned and asks, *"oh, so then you know I am Prince Daniel?"*. Amelia curtsies and smiles nodding as she looks at him in his casual clothes asking, *"what are you doing around these parts?"*. Daniel replies, *"I just needed some time to explore and relax, what about you?"*. Amelia replies, *"I come out here to relax too, it's so peaceful and calm here"*. Daniel tries to flirt and says, *"maybe we will keep meeting like this"*. Amelia blushes as she says, *"I would like that"*.

Daniel is stunned and surprised by Amelia's reaction as she laughs. Daniel thinks, *'her laugh is so cute;'* He then looks sadly as he asks, *"you want to keep meeting me because I'm the Prince, right?"*. She looks at him shocked and she shakes her head, *"no! not at all!"*. Daniel asks, *"then why do you want to meet me again?"*. Amelia comes closer, takes Daniel's hand, and shows her his hand as she asks, *"do you believe in fate?"*. He asks confused, *"fate?"*. She nods as she shows a line on his palm and replies, *"yes, fate, this line shows that you have met with me for a reason"*. Daniel looks at her as he asks, *"do you really believe in fate?"*. She smiles answering, *"perhaps, but I do know that I feel something special being here with you and I think you do too"*. Daniel smiles and comes closer as she turns to leave when he pulls her back and kisses her on the cheek. Amelia blushes as Daniel says, *" I'll see you tomorrow cutiepie"*. Over the next few months, Daniel and Amelia became closer, they looked forward to their meetings which were in secret; one afternoon Daniel and Amelia had a picnic near the lake as Amelia says, *"it's so lovely being here with you"*. Daniel laid his head on Amelia's lap, takes her hand kissing it as she feels butterflies.

Daniel smiles looking into her blue eye's saying, *"I love spending time with you cutiepie"*. Amelia kisses Daniel as she replies, *"me too"*. However, one day, Daniel and Amelia were caught together... Daniel brought Amelia to the stables as she fed and stroked Daniel's horse *'Snowy'*. Daniel says, *"Snowy is normally a fighter against everyone"*. Amelia laughs as she strokes him replying, *"Snowy's a real sweetheart"*. Daniel pulls Amelia closer, kisses her warmly as she wraps her arms around Daniel intensifying their kiss. They were both lost in the moment when a woman came into the stable and yelled, *"DANIEL!!!"*. Daniel and Amelia turn around shocked to see it is the Queen; Amelia curtsies as Daniel says, *"mom..."*. Queen Matilda asks, *"who is this girl?"*. Daniel replies, *"this is my girlfriend, Amy"*. Amelia blushes as she thinks, *'girlfriend?? why is my heart beating so fast right now?'*. Queen Matilda angrily yells, *"absolutely not! she cannot be your girlfriend; you are to marry either a noble or royal"*. Amelia looked sadly as she thought, *'why does my life feel like Cinderella right now?'*. Daniel asks, *"what about for love, mom?"*. Amelia tries to say something as Queen Matilda gives her a cold stare and tells her sternly, *"young lady, you must leave now!"*.

Amelia was stunned as she further says, *"you are not welcomed in or near my home peasant!"*. Daniel snaps angrily, *"MOM!"*. Amelia holds Daniel's arm as she calmly says, *"Danny, it's ok"*. Daniel turns back as he says, *"Amy-"*. Amelia smiles and says, *"talk to her, I'll see you later"*. Amelia leaves as Daniel turns back to his mom who coldly says, *"I forbid you from being with her"*. Daniel firmly replies, *"mom, you shall not I love her!"*. Queen Matilda rolls her eyes as she says, *"you love the IDEA of her, not her!"*. Daniel replies, *"you're wrong mom, I love her for who she is and with all my heart"*. Queen Matilda gives Daniel a stern look as she asks, *"really? son you are not allowed to be with her; look, she's not a royal or of noble blood, is she?"*. Daniel shakes his head and answers, *"no, she's not"*. Queen Matilda further says, *"and do you think people will respect you for marrying someone of less status than you?"*. Daniel replies, *"I don't care"*. Queen Matilda sighs as she says, *"son, you must marry into a noble family; this is non-negotiable, and you will not be given a choice in the matter. I suggest you go and say your goodbye to that girl"*.

Daniel heads to his room thinking about everything and feels, *'I have no choice'*. The next day, Daniel came to meet Amelia in the forest as she took a deep breath thinking, *'I can do this...'*. Daniel came over as he says, *"hi Amy"*. Amelia nervously replies, *"h-hey Danny"*. Daniel looks at her sadly saying, *"look, cutiepie I hate that I have to say this but-"*. Amelia interrupts Daniel as she says, *"please Danny, let me speak first"*. Daniel snaps at Amelia as he says, *"Amelia please! We can't do this anymore!"*. Amelia is hurt and asks, *"what are you talking about?"*. Daniel takes a deep breath replying, *"I have been forbidden from seeing you ever again; I don't want this, but I have a duty to my people. I hope you will someday understand if you don't now"*. Amelia looked at Daniel in silence as he said, *"please say something Amy"*. Amelia says, *"I love you"*. Daniel replies, *"I love you too and I hope I will see you again someday"*. He kisses her one last time before heading back; as she runs out of the forest and comes to an old cabin and begins to cry thinking, *'I couldn't do it... I couldn't tell him... I won't ever be able to tell him... I'm pregnant'*. She rubs her stomach thinking of Daniel and their moments together. She says talking to her baby, *"I know I am all alone... but I'm not because I have you and you will be my strength. Baby, keep me strong please, you won't ever meet your daddy, but I hope you are brave and kind-hearted just like him and as your mom, I promise to always be there for you".* Sixteen years later, it is early morning as Amelia says, *"Dawn! You have to get down here, now!".* Dawn gets up and changes as she yells, *"coming, mom!".* Dawn slides down the stair as she waves, *"morning, mom".* Amelia replies, *"good morning, Princess".*

Chapter 2

Dawn laughs as she says, *"mom, I grew out of that nickname years ago"*. Amelia says, *"I've always wanted you to feel like royalty"*. Dawn smiles as she says, *"aww mom, you've always made me feel like a royal, do I have to go to school?"*. Amelia rolls her eyes as she asks, *"must we always go through this child?"*. Dawn laughs as she winks playfully, *"I'm Princess mom, not a child"*. Amelia says, *"just go"*. Dawn grabs herself a snack as she hugs Amelia and heads out waving, *"bye mom, love you"*. Amelia replies, *"I love you too, Princess"*. Amelia thinks, *'I love you too, Princess Dawn'*. Soon at school, a young girl named Bethany says, *"there you are!"*; Dawn asks, *"how are you so bubbly and chirpy every single morning?"*. Bethany replies, *"coffee girl, just coffee"*. Dawn rolls her eyes as Bethany says, *"if you'd try it, you would like it"*.

Dawn nods as the tannoy above calls, *"Dawn, please come to the principal's office"*. Beth asks, *"what have you done?"*. Dawn replies, *"I hope nothing too serious"*. Dawn leaves and comes to the office as she asks, *"what have I done now?"*. Principal Mullins replies, *"Dawn, for once you are not in trouble this time"*. Dawn was stunned as she says, *"I'm not?"*. Principal Mullins says, *"Dawn, you're being excused for the rest of the day"*. Dawn was stunned as she asks, *"what? What do you mean?"*. Principal Mullins takes a deep breath and replies, *"Dawn, your mother is in the hospital, she was in a serious car accident on her way to work this morning"*. Dawn panics in shock and immediately runs out. Dawn comes to the hospital as she immediately asks the reception, *"which room is Amelia Warden in?"*. The staff replies, *"she's in the ICU"*. Dawn runs down the corridor as she comes to the ICU and sees a guard standing outside the door as she screams, *"GET OUT OF MY WAY, SIR!"*. The guard replies, *"I cannot allow you to enter"*. Dawn angrily asks, *"why not?"*. The guard replies, *"someone is in there"*. Dawn yells, *"you are going to let me in there NOW!!"*. The guard says, *"no chance, child"*. Dawn yells, *"I want to see my mother! she's in there!"*. The guard says, *"sorry, no can do!"*. Dawn yells, *"MOMMMMYY!!! I WANT TO SEE MY MOMMY!!"*. Daniel comes out as he asks, *"excuse me, is there a problem here?"*. Dawn yells, *"I WANT TO SEE MY MOTHER, NOW!"*. Daniel is stunned as he says, *"mother?!"*. Dawn angrily says, *"yes, my mother!"*. Daniel takes a deep breath and says, *"you are free to go"*. Dawn runs inside as she cries, *"mom!"*. Dawn looked at her mom's state as she saw the bruises, marks and also Amelia was wearing an oxygen mask. Dawn cried helplessly as she called out, *"mommy..."*. Just then Daniel came behind her as he says, *"I'm sorry, child"*. Dawn turns around as she yells angrily, *"who the hell are you and what are you doing here?"*.

Daniel gives a stern reply, *"I will not let you speak to King Daniel this way"*. Dawn is stunned by his response as she says confused, *"King Daniel??"*. He nods as Dawn takes a deep breath curtsying and says, *"Your highness... please forgive me"*. Daniel calmly says, *"it's alright child, I understand. Would you like me to call someone for you?"*. Dawn sadly replies, *"I have no one else except my mom"*. Daniel asks, *"what about your father?"*. Dawn replies, *"actually he left before I was born, I've never known him"*. Daniel says, *"hmm... how old are you child?"*. Dawn replies, *"I'm sixteen, Your Highness"*. Daniel looks at her for a moment as he thinks, *'no way! can it be possible? I mean, it can but-'*. Dawn turns to look at her mom as Daniel asks, *"have you ever met your father?"*. Dawn replies, *"no, Your Highness I have not"*. Dawn turns back to Daniel as she asks, *"Your Highness, I must ask... why does it matter to you?"*. He nervously says, *"I just... I'm just trying to figure out how to help you. that's all"*. Dawn cries and says, *"I appreciate it.."*. Daniel takes a deep breath as he asks, *"can I please ask you another question?"*. Dawn nods and answers, *"yes"*. Daniel asks, *"what is your name, child?, I don't think it's 'child' and I don't want to continue calling you that."* Dawn takes a deep breath as she replies, *"Dawn, Your Highness. My name is Dawn*

Sophia Warden. My mom told me when I was young that my middle name is her mom's name. I've never known or met any family members." Dawn cries as she says, "and now, I may lose my only family". Dawn wipes a tear, apologises to Daniel who says, "you don't need to apologise, you have every reason to cry". Dawn asks, "Your highness, can I ask you something please?". Daniel nods as Dawn asks, "why are you here? I know that you are the King, and you can do whatever you like, but why are you here? with my mom?". Daniel replies, "um... well your mother and I were friends a long time ago; I heard from someone that she was in an accident, and I wanted to check on her".

Dawn was stunned as she says, "my mom and you were friends?". Daniel nods and answers, "but as I said, it was many years ago". Dawn asks, "but then why did it matter for you to check on her?". Daniel replies, "because we were very close and I still love her as my friend and if she had ever come to me in need, I would gladly have helped her". Dawn thanks Daniel as he smiles; Dawn turns back to her mom as she says, "Your Highness, do you mind if I have some time alone with my mom?". Daniel replies, "of course not, Dawn. I'll be right outside if you need me." Dawn curtsies and thanks Daniel before turning back to her mom and speaking to her, "hi mom, I'm here for you and so is your friend, King Daniel. mom, I need you to fight and come back to me; I love you mom". She cries and leaves; later that afternoon Dawn comes to the garden as she cries when Daniel calls out to her, "Dawn". Dawn turns around as she waves, "hello, Your Highness". Daniel says, "you don't need to fake being okay". Dawn sighs wiping a tear as he continues, "I know what if feels like and I know you sometimes have to fake it". Daniel asks, "I've been meaning to ask you what's your plan?". Dawn replies, "I guess I will head home and do what I have to do." Daniel asks, "do you have someone to be with you to help you?". Dawn shakes her head as she replies, "no, it was just me and my mom". Daniel sympathises with her and says, "you shouldn't have to face this and be alone...". Dawn nods however replies, "I have no choice right now.. my mom would want me to be strong and manage the house; I must do what she needs right now". Daniel says, "at sixteen, you need someone to look after you". Dawn feels a little uncomfortable as she kindly says, "Your Highness, if you don't mind I really don't feel like I should speak to you about this. I need to inform my school about my decision to take some time out and sort things".

Daniel understands and nods saying, "let me give you my phone number so you can reach me if you need anything". Dawn gets emotional again asking, "Your Highness, why are you being so kind to me? I mean, I am nothing except the child of your friend." Daniel sighs answering, "Dawn.. I care deeply for your mom; and while I can't do anything for her, I can be there for you. it's the least I can do for the both of you". Dawn thanks Daniel as she turns to leave when he asks, "do you need a ride home?". Dawn smiles and replies, "I can manage thanks". However, Daniel insists as the driver drops Dawn home; she comes in and closes the door looking around. Dawn begins to cry and takes a photo frame as she holds it close thinking, 'mom I miss you so much... please come back to me.. I am so alone....'. Dawn stops crying for a moment as she thinks of her mom and decides to be strong; as she puts the photo down and thinks, 'I need to speak to Principal Mullins; I have to get a job now to pay for mom's medical bills and I need to be strong for her.'

Chapter 3

One week passes as Dawn gets up sadly thinking, *'mom is still not better... I need to finish getting some things in order.'* She takes a shower and heads downstairs to eat. Meanwhile, Ralph comes to the castle as he bows, *"Your Highness"*. Daniel says, *"Good morning Ralph"*. Ralph hands him an envelope and says, *"I have that number you have requested for and files"*. Daniel says, *"thank you"*. Ralph asks, *"Your Highness, if you don't mind... why do you wish to contact the royal lawyers? Has something happened?"*. Daniel replies, *"I just wanted to ask a law question"*. Ralph sighs as he says, *"I know that is not the case, however, I do trust you"*. Daniel thanks Ralph once again before he leaves as Daniel thinks, *'I hope this works.'* Daniel heads inside and makes a call as he says, *"hello, this is King Daniel speaking, I was wondering if you could assist me.. you see I have a question. It's regarding temporary guardianship of a minor"*. Later that afternoon; Dawn hears the doorbell ringing as she opens it to see Daniel standing outside.

Dawn curtsies as she says, *"Your Highness, how can I help you today?"*. Daniel replies, *"Dawn, I came to speak to you about some things and give you an offer"*. Dawn is a little reluctant as Daniel says, *"let me speak about the offer before you refuse"*. Dawn laughs as she nods; Daniel takes a deep breath, *"I have been trying to think of a way to help you out and I have a few ideas. How would you feel about coming to stay with me at the castle? It would just be until your mother has recovered"*. Dawn is surprised as she says, *"the castle?"*. Daniel nods as Dawn nervously replies, *"Your Highness, that's so kind of you to offer but I don't think I can accept it"*. Daniel is stunned by her response as he says, *"what? what do you mean, Dawn?"*. Dawn replies, *"I appreciate it, but I can't because that's too much, especially for you"*. Daniel asks, *"Is that really your answer?"*. Dawn nods as she says, *"I also plan to go back to school*

tomorrow... and start my new job." Daniel asks confused, *"new job?".*
Dawn nods as she says, *"I need to work to pay for my mom's medical bill,
I am happy to do it; all my life she has done everything for me".* Daniel
smiles as he says, *"you remind me so much of Amelia when she was young;
she was optimistic and strong".* Dawn thanks him as he says, *"I would
still like you to come with me to the castle, I don't mind taking you to
school and work".* Dawn hesitated for a moment as she says, *"that's a lot
to ask from you".* Daniel nods answering, *"I know but I would happily
do it".* Dawn decides to accept the offer as she heads to her room to
pack; Dawn heads to the bathroom as Daniel comes into Dawn's room
looking around thinking, *'I have to be fast... I just need to find Dawn's
birth certificate, maybe it will have what I am looking for on it...'.* Daniel
comes into the closet and opens the drawer trying to look for the paper
just then Dawn comes in shocked to see Daniel going through her
belongings. She asks, *"what the hell do you think you are doing in here?".*
Daniel gets up startled and replies, *"um.. actually, your mother borrowed
something from me years ago and I wanted to see if it was still here".*

Dawn doesn't buy Daniel's reason as she sternly says, *"you're lying!
how dare you come in here and lie to me! you act as if you want to help me
but you're not!".* Daniel tries to calm her down however she says, *"Leave!
Get out now!".* Daniel tries to explain saying, *"Dawn, please!"* She grabs
his arm, pushes him to the front door and yells, *"GET OUT!!!!".* Daniel
leaves as Dawn locks her door and angrily wondering, *'who the hell
does he think he is? He had no right going through mine or my mom's
belonging! I don't care if he claimed to know my mother years ago!'.* Dawn
sighs as she takes her mom's photo frame and begins to cry; later that
evening, Dawn cooked her dinner and also prayed for her mother's
recovery. The next day, Dawn awoke and got ready for school; Bethany
sees Dawn as she excitedly says, *"OMG girl! you're back. How are you
coping?".* Dawn tries to be strong however sadly replies, *"I'm missing my
mom Beth... but I need to be strong for her; I've got a part-time job after
school".*

Bethany was surprised as she asks, "*what do you mean you have got a job?*". Dawn rolls her eyes as she replies, *"I am reliable, responsible, and mature."* Bethany laughs as she gives Dawn an encouraging and supportive hug. However, just then the tannoy says, *"DAWN WARDEN, PLEASE COME TO THE PRINCIPAL'S OFFICE IMMEDIATELY"*. Dawn panics again as Bethany calms her down and wishes her luck. Dawn immediately heads to Principal Mullin's office as she takes a deep breath and opens the door. She is shocked to see Daniel smiling at her as she asks, *"what are YOU doing here?"*. Principal Mullins says, *"Dawn, this is not the way to speak to King Daniel"*. Dawn rolls her eyes as Principal Mullins apologizes on Dawn's behalf. Daniel looks at Principal Mullins saying, *"do not worry about it"*. Daniel turns to look back at Dawn as he says, *"Dawn, yesterday I tried to be nice to you, but now? you have left me with no choice! You are to leave this school immediately and come with me to the castle"*.

Chapter 4

Dawn yells, *"WHAT???!"*. Principal Mullins says, *"Dawn, please-"*. Dawn says, *"no, I don't want to hear it! you have absolutely no reason to come into my life like this!"*. Daniel says, *"Dawn-"*. Dawn yells, *"SHUT UP!!"*. Principal Mullins says, *"Dawn Warden!"*. Dawn says angrily, *"I don't give a damn anymore! first, my mom is injured and then you come in and try to take over EVERYTHING! What gives you the right?!"* Daniel hands her a file saying, *"these do ok!"*. Dawn is stunned as she says, *"what?!"*. She has a look at it while Daniel says, *"I am now your temporary legal guardian"*. Dawn is not impressed as she says, *"you've got to be joking??"*. Daniel replies, *"no, I'm not"*. Dawn says, *"I need to step out for a minute, now if you'll excuse me..."*. Dawn comes out as Daniel looks sad whilst Principal Mullins tries to apologize to him. Daniel says, *"I knew this wouldn't go well with her"*. In the girl's lavatory Dawn is crying her eyes out as Bethany asks, *"Dawn! what's the wrong girl?"* Bethany hugs Dawn as she replies, *"you have no idea..."*. Bethany says, *"talk to me Dawn, tell me what's going on?"*. Dawn says, *"Beth, there's just so much going on right now. I'm just really overwhelmed."* Bethany notices something is wrong as she asks, *"Dawn, something tells me this is far more than you being overwhelmed... there is, isn't there?"*. Dawn thinks, *'I can't tell her the whole truth... not yet'*.

Dawn takes a deep breath as she says, *"someone from my mom's past is trying to come in and help me out; but I don't know if I trust him. and now, he's removing me from school without a reason"*. Bethany was stunned as she says, *"he's removing you from school?"*. Dawn nods as Bethany ask, *"how well do you know this guy?"*. Dawn replies, *"hardly, I didn't even know he was friends with my mom until I met him at the hospital"*. Bethany asks, *"why do you think he's removing you from school?"*. Dawn replies, *"I don't know"*. Bethany says, *"I think something is up"*. Dawn nods replying, *"I think you might be right and there's some kind of ulterior motive behind this."* Bethany asks, *"Dawn, what do you think it is? What do you think you're going to do?"*. Dawn replies *"not sure, but he's my temporary legal guardian now..."*. Bethany was shocked as she says, *"what?! So does that mean you have no choice?"*.

Dawn shakes her head answering, *"I guess not but I am going to go back out and make demands"*. Bethany gives her another hug and wishes her luck as Dawn says, *"I'll text you once I get home tonight, ok?"*. Dawn leaves the bathroom and comes back to the principal's office as she apologizes and says, *"I am willing to go with you- but under some conditions of my own"*. Daniel nods saying, *"sure"*. Dawn says, *"first thing- Principal Mullins, can we please speak in private?"*. Principal Mullins was stunned as Dawn says, *"he's my legal guardian and this discussion is something for me and him, not you"*. Daniel turns to Principal Mullins saying, *"it's ok, thank you for working with me."* Principal Mullins gets up and leaves the room as Daniel turns back to Dawn asking, *"okay, what's up?"*. Dawn replies, *"I am not happy about this or how you did this- but we are now stuck in this, so here it goes, I will go with you."* Daniel smiles and nods as she says, *"but you must take me to see my mom AND I must be allowed to stay at my home. I have to work still, and I want to be at home to make the journey easier to work"*. Daniel says, *"Oh...um...well... I've paid for your mom's medical bill"*. Dawn was shocked as she asks, *"what?!"*. Daniel answers, *"I just wanted to help her out"*. Dawn says, *"Your Highness, that was far too kind of you"*. Daniel says, *"well it's all sorted, so you don't have to work"*. Dawn says, *"my condition to stay in my house is still the same."* Daniel says, *"hmm... that can be arranged under the agreement that you let a guard stay with you"*. Dawn rolls her eyes as she says, *"if I have to.."*. Dawn says, *"so if you're removing me from school today, can I please go see my mom?"*. Daniel nods as she asks, *"I have one more question.... What am I going to do for school?"*. Daniel replies, *"I guess I will hire a tutor for you. you can study at home"*.

Dawn is sad as he says, *"we will discuss soon. For now, you are out of school for the rest of the week, and I will take you to see your mom"*. Dawn nods as they get to the hospital; Dawn talks to her mom however she soon runs out crying as Daniel asks, *"Dawn, are you ok?"*. Dawn turns to Daniel replied, *"I just don't get why she isn't waking up"*. Daniel says, *"Dawn, head injuries are hard to deal with and it will take time for her to recover. However, the doctor sees activity in her scans, therefore there is hope she will come out of this"*. Dawn nods as Daniel notice that something else is troubling her as he asks, *"what's bothering you?"*. Dawn replies, *"look Your Highness, I appreciate everything you've done for me and my mom, but you're not telling me something and I am not sure why. it's so overwhelming too and I still don't know why you are so interested in me and my mom. It's really starting to upset me, and I cannot take it, my whole life is a mess right now and you really aren't helping"*. Daniel says, *"Dawn, I'm so sorry, I didn't know."* She says, *"please I want to know why"*. Daniel thinks, *'I need to tell her about my doubts'*. Daniel says, *"Dawn... I need to tell you something but let's go somewhere more private"*. Dawn nods and goes with Daniel to a private room as she says, *"ok, tell me..."*. Daniel takes a deep breath saying *"um... Dawn... I am not sure how to say this... but I think I might be your father"*.

Chapter 5

D awn is shocked by Daniel's words as she asks, *"what? how?"*. Daniel replies, *"I mean, I figured you would already know this with your mom and all"*. Dawn replies, *"no! that's not what I mean. How can you be my, father? You and mom were friends, right?"*. Daniel nods as he replies, *"we were far more than friends, at one point your mom and I were in love"*. Dawn asks, *"really?"*. Daniel nods answering, *"yep, madly even. I never married because I never fell out of love with her, but I did fall out of touch; but when I heard she was in an accident, I had to come and see her. that's how I met you."* Dawn asks, *"so, why didn't you tell me straightaway?"*. Daniel replies, *"I didn't want to tell you anything until I knew you were mine."* Dawn asks, *"and how are we supposed to find out?"*. Daniel replies, *"I mean, I was going to do a paternity test"*. Dawn rolls her eyes as she asks, *"and how would you do that without asking me?"*. Daniel replies, *"I guess I hadn't quite thought about that"*. Dawn says, *"I think we need to discuss a paternity test."* Daniel nods saying, *"moreover, I've thought I never had any kids of my own, so my heirs are my niece and nephew; however, if you are my child, then you are the heir to the throne"*. Dawn is stunned as she says, *"I'm sorry, what?!"*. Daniel says, *"that's why I haven't said anything, I wanted to make absolutely sure that you were mine first. That's why I was in your closet the other day trying to find a birth certificate or something that would say I'm your dad."* Dawn says, *"you should have told me this from the beginning, I haven't even had a chance to wrap my head around this! okay... look I need to go home and just think about everything."*

Daniel nods as he says, *"I totally understand."* They soon head out as Dawn comes home and sees a guy in the living room as she asks, *"who are you?!"*. He bows as he replies, *"I am Raphael, your personal guard but you can call me Ralph"*. Dawn says, *"oh....okay"*. Ralph says, *"I am here to help and protect you, Dawn."* Dawn nods as she asks, *"wait, how do you know my name?".* Ralph replies, *"the King informed me."* Dawn sighs as Ralph asks, *"are you ok?".* Dawn replies *"I'm sorry... I'm just way too stressed out to talk right now".* Ralph understands as Dawn says, *"I am feeling really...um. Please excuse me".* She immediately runs upstairs to her room as Ralph wonders, *'was it something I said?'.* Dawn breaks down in her room as Ralph knocks on the door calling, *"Dawn?".* Dawn says, *"please leave me alone, Ralph".* Ralph says, *"look, I am here to protect you."* Dawn says *"Ralph, you can't protect me from my feelings".* Ralph says, *"I mean, I can always try".* Dawn laughs as he says, *"I'd like to try?".* Dawn asks, *"how?".* Ralph asks, *"may I come in please?".*

Dawn opens the door as Ralph asks, *"were you crying?".* Dawn replies, *"yeah, I was. I'm sorry but you have no idea".* Ralph says, *"no, I don't but I'd like to know what you're going through."* Dawn asks, *"do you even know who I am and why you're here?".* Ralph replies, *"well, the King has informed me that you may be his daughter and he wants you protected until he is sure."* Dawn was surprised as she says, *"I guess you do know".* Ralph says, *"kind of helps being the King's right-hand man".* Dawn looks at Ralph as he says, *"I have an idea...".* Dawn asks, *"what's your idea?".* Ralph says, *"well, I would like to order us pizza and watch a movie- of your choice and I won't even complain if it's a chick flick."* Dawn smiles and replies, *"you know, what? that sounds like a wonderful idea".* Ralph says, *"I agree, I'll order the pizza and you choose the movie".* Ralph leaves as Dawn wonders, *'wow he's really nice and cute...'.* A few moments later, Ralph says *,"Dawn!".* Dawn comes downstairs replying, *"what is it, Ralph?".* Ralph says, *"pizza's ready! Have you chosen the movie?".* Dawn nods replying, *"yes, we're going to watch Spiderman No Way Home".* Ralph excitedly says, *"I love that movie!".* The next morning, Dawn's phone rings early as she gets up and answers, *"hello?".* Daniel says, *"Good morning, it's King Daniel. I'm sorry if I woke you up".* Dawn replies, *"well, you did. But I didn't think that's why you called me."* Daniel replies, *"no,*

I called you to get ready, we are going to the hospital to take that paternity test." she says, *"already?"*. Daniel says, *"yes, I'll be there in an hour"*.

Dawn ends the call, heads for a shower and changes as she thinks, *'ready to find out if I'm a princess or not....'*. A few hours later in the hospital are the tests are done. Daniel asks, *"doctor, when will we find out the results?"*. The doctor replies *"it takes around three weeks"*. Daniel nods as he says, *"I also expect you will keep this entire thing a secret?"*. The doctor bows and nods as he looks at Dawn asking *"Dawn, do you have any questions?"*. Dawn asks, *"how will we find out about the results? Like a call or do we come back in?"*. The doctor says, *"we will read the results here"*. Daniel nods as the doctor heads out leaving Daniel and Dawn to talk. Daniel asks, *"how are you feeling right now Dawn?"*. Dawn replies, *"really overwhelmed, my brain is going a million miles a minute"*. Daniel laughs, *"I can imagine, I don't know if it will ever get easier either. However, if you are my daughter, I will be there to help you in every way I can."* Dawn thanks him as they soon drive home, however, the moment Dawn steps home she is shocked to see a familiar face.

Chapter 6

Dawn asks, *"what are you doing here?"*. Bethany rolled her eyes replying, *"it's good to see you too, Dawn"*. Ralph says, *"she claims to know you"*. Bethany angrily says, *"I DO!"*. Daniel says, *"Dawn, stay behind me!"*. Dawn rolls her eyes as she says, *"seriously, she's not going to hurt anyone, this is my bestie, Bethany"*. Bethany says, *"I told you so!"*. Daniel had doubts looking at Bethany saying, *"I still don't trust you"*. Bethany looks at Daniel for a moment as she soon says shocked, *"OMG! YOU'RE KING DANIEL!!"*. Bethany bows as she apologizes saying, *"Your Highness, what an honor to be in your presence!"*. Bethany looks at Dawn asking nervously, *"um...Dawn, why is King Daniel here?"*. Daniel says, *"Dawn, I need to head out, but I'll speak to you later"*. Dawn nods as he leaves with Ralph looking at her saying, *"um... I think you're safe here Dawn, I will take my leave too"*. He bows as he leaves the room as Bethany gives Dawn a cold stare, Dawn soon heads to her room with Bethany. Bethany asks, *"what the hell is going on?!"*. Dawn is reluctant to answer replying, *"um.. remember the man I told you that came into my life recently?"*. Bethany says, *"Damn, It's King Daniel! Why didn't you tell me?"*. Dawn replies, *"look, honestly Beth, I have far too much on the mind than to have an argument with you."* Bethany takes a deep breath apologizing saying, *"look I'm shocked and confused, you have to understand..."*. Dawn nods as Bethany change her expression asking, *"who's the hottie you're now living with?"*.

Dawn rolls her eyes saying, *"really, Beth?"*. Bethany looks at her replying, *"what? he's so hot and lush! I call dibs"*. Dawn laughs saying, *"you're silly! You can have him"*. Bethany smiles saying, *"cool, he's mine, his choice will be me."* Dawn says, *"oh Beth, I've missed you, but you know he can make his own decisions?"*. Bethany says, *"I've missed you more girl, we should have a girl's night!"*. Dawn is hesitant as Bethany is surprised by her response asking, *"you're always up for a girl's night?"*. Dawn sadly replies, *"I've been really sad and overwhelmed lately, I don't want to ruin your fun"*. Bethany comes over and gives her a hug saying, *"Dawn, it's my job as your bestie to cheer you up and make you feel better. What do you say?"*. Dawn nods as Bethany comes down to put on the movie, *'After'*. Later that evening, Bethany talks about Tessa and Hardin as Dawn yawns replying, *"sorry I am just so tired"*. Bethany says, *"maybe we should call it a night. Are you sure you'll be okay alone?"*. Dawn replies, *"I am not alone; Ralph is here with me"*. Bethany says, *"remember he's mine!"*.

Dawn laughs replying, *"you silly goofball, sure ok he's yours!"*. Bethany leaves but not before promising to visit again tomorrow. Bethany soon leaves as Dawn gets back to her deep thoughts as she wonders, *'could mom have left something for Daniel? Maybe I should check it out'*. Dawn heads into the closet as she looks through the drawers and finds a letter addressed to Daniel; she opens it and reads as she begins to cry thinking, *'Oh mom, you were pregnant with me, and you never got the chance to tell Daniel. She was so afraid to tell him! I need to let Daniel know about this.'* Dawn grabs her phone as she calls Daniel who answers, *"hello Dawn, is everything ok?"*. Dawn replies, *"hi Daniel, sorry to call you late but I have something to show you. can you come and see me tomorrow morning?"*. Daniel replies, *"sure, I will come by tomorrow, Good night"*. Dawn ends the call as she thinking, *'God, I feel so overwhelmed right now; I should get some sleep'*. The next morning, Daniel comes as Ralph opens the door surprised to see him; Ralph bows as he asks, *"are you ok this morning, Your Highness?"* Daniel replies, *"I'm exhausted but otherwise fine"*. Ralph advises him more rest as Daniel nods replying, *"once this whole matter with Dawn is dealt with, I will"*. Dawn comes there as she says, "Good morning, Daniel". Ralph and Daniel say, *"Good morning, Dawn";* she smiles as she looks at Daniel saying, *"Daniel, I have some things to show you"*. Ralph excuses himself to the kitchen as Dawn brings Daniel back to her room. Daniel asks, *"how has Ralph been since staying with you?"*. Dawn replies, *"I barely see him".* Daniel nods asking, *"what is it that you wanted to show me?".* Dawn sighs as she brings out the letter and book replying, *"so, it's a lot of stuff, but this is the first thing".*

Daniel reads the letter as he says, *"your mom wrote this for me...".* Dawn nods nervously as Daniel says, *"when she was pregnant with you.. to tell me that you were mine...".* Daniel is stunned as Dawn calmly says, *"you can't be surprised".* Daniel says, *"don't get me wrong Dawn, I had a doubt, but I didn't think that you truly were.. I'm just... stunned and surprised".* Dawn laughs as she says, *"I'd love to be that person, but the paternity test needs to come back first."* Daniel nods in agreement as he says, *"but I think at this point, it's clear to me you are my daughter, and I would like to bring you home with me."* Dawn's facial expression widen with excitement as she asks, *"you mean at the castle?".* Daniel nods asking, *"would you like to come with me to the castle?".*

Chapter 7

Dawn smiles replying, *"I'd love to!"*. As they share a hug, Daniel says, *"I am so happy to have met you, sweetie"*. Dawn smiles nodding replying, *'dad'*. Daniel smiles as he says, *"I like it when you call me dad, but we need to keep this matter private."* Dawn asks, *"why?"*. Daniel replies, *"don't get me wrong Dawn, we have to wait for the results; once we know for sure, you and I can announce it together, along with some hostile response from at least one member of my family. Bear in mind, my nephew Charlie is supposed to take over the throne since I didn't have an heir myself; but now, I do."* Dawn smiles as she hands Daniel a book saying, *"mom, left this for you too. It will be more sentimental to you"*. Daniel opens the book thinking, *'it's a book from Amelia to me... wow she's describing every moment of Dawn's life...'*. After reading it, Daniel looks at Dawn thanking her as she smiles saying, *"I hope those stories can now start including you"*. Daniel nods and hugs her once more before saying, *"I think it's time you start getting stuff packed to go, I'll asl Ralph to help you out."*

Dawn nods as later after breakfast; Dawn began to pack her things in a box as she looked around feeling sad. Ralph came in as she took a deep breath to face him; he asked, *"Dawn, are you ok?"*. Dawn smiles replying, *"I'm fine Ralph"*. Ralph notices Dawn's sadness as he says, *"if you'd ever need to talk, I'm a really good listener"*. Dawn thanks him as he says, *"well, we need to start packing if you want to move to the castle by tomorrow morning"*. Bethany comes in as she says stunned, *"you're moving to the castle?"*. Dawn nodded nervously as Bethany asks, *"why are you moving to the castle? What are you hiding from me, Dawn?"*. She replies nervously, *"um...er...I...well.."*. Ralph says, *"Dawn might be King Daniel's daughter, so he has decided to move her into the castle"*. Bethany is shocked as she says, *"you've got to be kidding me!!"*. Ralph leaves the room as Dawn yells, *"YOU'RE SUCH A SPOILSPORT RALPH!"*. Ralph replies, *"that's fine with me!"*. Bethany looks at Dawn with a shocked expression asking, *"you might be a princess? really, how could you not tell me? I am your best friend!"*. Dawn replies *"sorry Beth, I wasn't allowed to tell anyone, Daniel didn't want me to and honestly, I didn't know I was until a few days ago."* Bethany rolls her eyes and gives an annoyed expression as Dawn apologizes. Dawn says, *"I could really use your help packing my stuff"*.

Bethany smiles as they both begin to pack bags and boxes. Bethany asks, *"Dawn, are you going to do a DNA test or something?"*. Dawn replies, *"it's a paternity test which was done yesterday and takes three weeks to get the results"*. Bethany nods saying, *"promise me I will be the first to know!"* Dawn promises as they share a hug; a few hours later Bethany leaves as Dawn is in the living room when Ralph comes over asking, *"Dawn, have you done all your packing?"*. Dawn gives Ralph a cold expression replying, *"how could you do that?! I would have told Beth the truth myself"*. Ralph says, *"no you wouldn't, be honest Dawn you're still processing what's been happening lately, and I know later on you would instantly regret lying to your friend"*. Dawn looks at Ralph sadly as he says, *"look, Dawn, I'm sorry please don't be sad; how about I take you for ice-cream. Your choice of any place and ice-cream flavor"*. Dawn cheers up as they soon head out; as the evening falls they head over to the harbor as Dawn says, *"ok, I've forgiven you for earlier, the ice cream was tasty; I just love Ben & Jerry Phish food"*. Dawn suddenly feels a little emotional as she asks, *"Ralph, what's the castle like?"*. Ralph replies, *"it's beautiful and also very busy; you will enjoy everything there. what do you plan to do on your arrival?"*. Dawn replies, *"I am not sure, Ralph"*. Ralph senses Dawn's sadness in her tone asking, *"Dawn, are alright? What's wrong?"*. Dawn begins to cry telling Ralph her feelings of being scared and overwhelmed. Ralph says, *"Dawn, I am so sorry you feel so much!"*. Dawn apologizes for crying as Ralph comes over embracing her and says *"Dawn, I will always be by your side and promise to be there for you."* Dawn smiles as she says, *"thanks Ralph, you're a great friend"*.

Ralph and Dawn soon head home as she wishes him goodnight; the next morning Ralph waits for Dawn in the living room as he wonders, *'if King Daniel ever found out I hugged his daughter, I could be in deep trouble, but it felt right to embrace her. I can't explain it like why does it make me feel comfortable? I hate seeing sadness and tears in her eyes. She's had so much happened to her, and she needed a friend. but why does it feel like I've crossed a line? Could I have feelings for Dawn? Oh no! I might! I might have feelings for her... I have to ignore my feelings... she's beautiful and lovely.. yes I might be drawn to her, but she must never know....'*

Chapter 8

Dawn comes downstairs as she looks around the house; Ralph comes over to her asking, *"Dawn, are you ok?"*. Dawn takes a deep breath replying, *"yep.. just thinking when I'll get to see this place again"*. Ralph says, *"I'm sure his Highness will let you come here as you please"*. Dawn says, *"sure, maybe... thank you, Ralph"*. Ralph smiles asking, *"are you sure you're ok? is there anything you want to talk about?"*. Dawn replies, *"I am feeling nervous but also excited"*. The door opens to King Daniel as Ralph bows and greets Daniel; Daniel asks, *"Ralph, can I please have a moment alone with Dawn?"*. Ralph nods, *"of course, sir, I'll be waiting in the car."* Daniel looks at Dawn asking, *"are you ready to go home?"*. Dawn nods as she answers, *"I'm just telling myself that the castle will be my new home now"*. Daniel asks, *"why's that?"*. Dawn replies, *"dad, this has always been my home, the memories are here, and I don't know how to imagine another place as home."* Dawn gets emotional as Daniel says, *"sweetie, I'm not going to pretend I understand what you're going through, but I promise you I will always be there for you and if you are my child, I will do everything I can to support you in every way"*.

Dawn thanks Daniel as she says, *"I'm just a little stressed out and overwhelmed"*. Daniel gives her a hug as they soon head out; they soon drive to the castle. Daniel and Dawn look outside as Daniel says, *"welcome home, Dawn"*. They come inside as Dawn is amazed by the decoration and interior as she says, *"wow! This castle is incredible"*. Daniel thanks her as he says, *"this is your home too, let me take you to your room"*. They head upstairs as Daniel opens a door as Dawn sees a silk bed with curtains and beautiful wallpaper and floor. Dawn asks surprised, *"is this mine?! thank you, I love it!"*. Daniel asks, *"is there anything I can do to help you settle in and make it feel more like home?"*. Dawn says, *"dad, you've already done so much for me; I wish you could bring my mom home".* Daniel looks sad replying, *"I wish I could too, princess".* Dawn is stunned to hear Daniel call her, *'Princess'.* Daniel asks, *"what's wrong?".* Dawn sadly replies, *"this is what my mom calls me... her little princess".* Daniel smiles saying, *"well, I like this name for you, and you might actually be a princess. It will take a little time to get used to your new title."* Daniel looks at the time as he says, *"I have a few things to attend to, but would you like to grab some dinner tonight?".* Dawn asks, *"don't you have a chef to cook for you?".* Daniel laughs replying, " *of course I do, but sometimes you just want to eat an Italian pizza or Chinese special. What do you think?".* Dawn smiles saying, *"pizza sounds fantastic!".* Daniel leaves as Dawn looks around wondering, *'maybe I should explore the castle?'.* She walks out of the room down the corridor. Meanwhile, in the living room, Charlie and Daphne are talking as Charlie wonders *'who is she?',* Dawn comes into the room as Daphne says, *"brother, I cannot wait- brother? What are you looking at? Who's she?".* Daphne turns as she sees Dawn and replies, *"I don't know brother, but let's find out!".* Daphne yells, *"HELLO THERE!".* Dawn comes over and waves as Daphne and Charlie both say, *'hi'.* Charlie asks, *"I've never seen you here before, who are you?".* Dawn thinks, *'gotta lie... don't tell them the truth!'.* Dawn replies, *"hi I'm Dawn".* Daphne asks, *"are you're a new help?".* Dawn replies *"no... um I'm actually a friend of the king".* Charlie is surprised as Daphne says, *"that's sensational I guess! What are you doing here in the castle?".* Dawn sadly says, *"my mom is in the hospital and she's the King's friend, she's asked if he can look after me for a while until she gets better".* Daphne sympathetically says, *"it's so sad to hear that Dawn! Nevertheless, I am so happy to have another girl in the castle! Charlie is such a drag".* Dawn asks, *"Prince Charlie?",* Charlie smiles, *"I'm glad to see you know me".* Charlie and Daphne have a little tiff as Dawn asks nervously, *"P-Princess Daphne?".* Daphne nods as Dawn says excitedly, *"I can't believe I'm meeting with the Royal niece and nephew of the King!".* Daphne giggles saying, *"please Dawn, call me Daphne who knows we could be friends!".*

Charlie looks at Dawn suspiciously as he says, *"I don't believe you!"*. Daphne asks, *"why not?"*. Charlie shrugs his shoulder and soon leaves. Daphne says, *"please ignore Charlie, he was born a pompous ass"*. Dawn laughs as Ralph soon enters greeting, *"Princess Daphne, Dawn"*. He bows as he passes a message to Daphne who soon leaves the room; Ralph looks at Dawn nervously as she waves, *"hey Ralph"*. Ralph says, *"hey Dawn, how do you feel about the castle so far?"*. Dawn replies, *"I love it! it's so incredible and everyone seems so friendly!"*. Ralph smiles, *"that's good! I'm glad you're happy here"*. Dawn says, *"I've met Prince Charlie and Princess Daphne; I don't think Prince Charlie likes me"*. Ralph reassures Dawn asking, *"would you like to go for a walk? I was hoping to take you through the garden"*. Dawn smiles nodding as they soon head out; Dawn looks at the flowers and water fountain in amazement. Dawn says *"Ralph, this garden is magnificent!"*. Ralph says *"yeah, the Queens like to keep them looked after"*. Dawn says, *"I've been wondering about that... how can the Queen be Queen if Daniel is the King?"*. Ralph replies, *"the Queen stepped down from power to let King Daniel rule"*. Dawn asks, *"is the Queen here?"*. Ralph replies *"no, she lives at a country-house however occasionally she does visit"*. Dawn takes a deep breath saying, *"I hope she likes me"*. Ralph assures her she will be loved as Ralph checks on Dawn asking, *"are you sure you're ok?"*. Dawn nods replying *"yep, but I'm still nervous and trying to battle my nerves"*. Ralph again reassures her as Dawn thinks, *'he's hugged me before... why isn't he hugging me now?'*. Dawn asks, *"have I done something wrong, Ralph?"*. Ralph looks stunned as she says, *"what?"*. Dawn sadly says, *"if I have done anything wrong please tell me.. you hugged me last night, and I feel like since you did, you've been distant with me. I just wanted to make sure that I haven't done anything wrong"*. Ralph takes a deep breath replying, *"Dawn, you have done nothing wrong, I may have because if you are who we think you are... the princess.. I cannot hug you.. I am not of your status or level and therefore I cannot touch you"*.

Chapter 9

Three weeks passed; Dawn settled in the castle making friends with Daphne however Charlie was still doubtful; Ralph kept his distance from Dawn since their last conversation. Early the next morning, Dawn wakes up as she eats breakfast with Daniel who asks, *"Dawn, are you ready for this afternoon?"* Dawn nods as Charlie and Daphne soon come in to eat. Dawn finishes her breakfast and heads upstairs for a quick shower and grabs a book until she sees the time and it's 1PM; Daniel asks, *"Dawn! Are you ready to go?"*. Dawn slides down the stair as they head out into the limo; Dawn felt nervous as Daniel looked at her asking, *"are you alright, Dawn?"*. Dawn looks at Daniel replying, *"I'm not sure.. I just... I... I'm nervous.. what if I am not your daughter? What if I am? what happens next?"*.

Daniel takes a deep breath as he says, *"Dawn, if you're not my daughter, you will still stay with me until your mom's better; but I think we both know that you are my daughter, and this result is just a formality"*. Dawn smiles nervously as Daniel assures her that he is here and not to worry; they finally reach the hospital as the limo stops with Daniel asking, *"Dawn, are you ready for this?"*. Dawn nods replying, *"I guess so..."*. They come to the room as the doctor bows and greets Daniel as the doctor asks, *"are you both ready for the results?"*. Daniel and Dawn both reply together, *"yes"*. The doctor opens an envelope reading, *"as the result here shows, congratulations Dawn is, without doubt, your daughter"*. Daniel smiles excitedly as the doctor says, *"I will give you a few minutes to talk"*. Daniel asks, *"Dawn, how are you feeling now since finding out I am your dad?"*. Dawn excitedly replies, *"I am so happy and feeling ecstatic"*. They share a hug as Daniel says, *"now you're certainly my daughter, Princess Dawn... the question is how do we declare you?"*. Dawn was stunned asking, *"declare me?"*. Daniel replies, *"you're the rightful heir to the throne and we need to declare you to everyone"*. Dawn felt nervous as Daniel says, *"you'll be fine Princess, I will be by your side"*. Dawn asks worriedly, *"won't Charlie be mad?";* Daniel looks at Dawn answering, *"even if he is, it doesn't matter because you are the rightful heir, it is your birthright and if he will be mad, he will soon get over it"*. Dawn nods as Daniel still taking in the joy says, *"I can't believe, after all these years I have a child. You'll be an amazing princess; let's hold a party for tomorrow"*. Dawn was a little worried about it being tomorrow as Daniel gave her another hug assuring her it was going to be ok. Dawn asks, *"dad, how fancy will this party be? I don't really have any fancy outfits"*.

Daniel replies, *"we can go shopping, Princess"*. Dawn cheers happily asking, *"can I invite Beth to the party tomorrow, dad?"*. Daniel nods as Dawn hugs him happily thanking him. Daniel and Dawn head out to shop and also eat lunch as Dawn thinks, *'I am so blessed to have my dad with me';* they head home as Dawn calls Bethany informing her of the results as Bethany is super happy. Dawn asks, *"Beth, please keep it a secret? also, tomorrow there's a party at the castle."* Bethany replies, *"of course, bestie I will keep your secret and see you tomorrow"*. Later that afternoon, Dawn came into the garden as she saw Ralph. She nervously said, *"oh, hi Ralph"*. He says, *"hi, how are you, Dawn?"*. Dawn replies, *"I'm ok, how are you?"*. Ralph replies, *"I'm fine, do you... do you know if you are a princess or not?"*. Dawn takes a deep breath replying, *"I do, and I am"*. Ralph look sadly down as he thought, *'of course, she's the princess...'.* Dawn noticed Ralph in deep thoughts as she called, *"RALPH?"*. Ralph says, *"sorry, congratulations, Princess"*. He bows as Dawn says, *"it still feels so surreal.. I mean other people addressing me as Princess."* Ralph asks, *"what do you mean?"*. Dawn answers, *"well my mom she used to call me Princess, I never felt like one but now I am one"*. Ralph bows as he says, *"well, enjoy the rest of your day, Princess"*. Ralph turns to leave as Dawn calls out, *"wait a second! Ralph!"*. Ralph stops and turns to ask, *"what is it, Princess?"*. Dawn answers, *"we are going to have a party tomorrow to announce me and I wondered if you'd like to come".* Ralph says, *"I'm already coming, not for fun! I'm working".* Dawn felt sad as he continued, *"it's one of the many tasks I do as your father's right-hand man. I'm sure I'll see you around, Princess."* Ralph leaves as Dawn thinks, *'why am I so sad that he has to work through the party? I know he'll be there.. I wish we could have waited until mom was ok... I hope I can make dad proud tomorrow'.*

Chapter 10

The next evening, Dawn was in her room as she thought, *'today's the day of the royal party... God I'm so nervous'*. Soon there was a knock on the door as Dawn yells, *"enter, Beth!"*. Bethany enters as she says, *"hey, Princess!"*. Dawn rolls her eyes as Bethany excitedly says, *"I can't help it! finding out my bestie is a Princess!"*. Dawn says, *"look no one knows except you, Daniel, Ralph, and me ok?"*. Bethany asks, *"Ralph knows?"*. Dawn nods replying, *"yeah, he's Daniel's, right-hand man"*. Bethany asks, *"Daniel told him?"*. Dawn answers, *"no, I did; he found me in the garden and asked me"*. Bethany asks, *"why wouldn't Daniel share with him that information?"*. Dawn rolls her eyes replying, *"I'm not sure, but he came to me, and I trust him"*. Bethany gives Dawn a playful smirk saying, *"he's a hottie; you've got to admit!"*. Dawn says nervously, *"um... well he isn't bad I guess"*. Bethany says, *"you DO like him!"*. Dawn gives Bethany a serious look as she says, *"I like his presence, ok."* Dawn laughs as she asks, *"are you ready to get dressed for the party?"*. Bethany replies, *"since, you won't talk about your toy-boy, guess no choice"*. Daphne comes in asking, *"you have a toyboy, Dawn?"*. Dawn replies, *"Beth, here is my bestie and she seems to think so"*. Daphne comes over asking for an explanation as Bethany instantly recognizes Princess Daphne. Bethany immediately curtsies as Daphne says, *"no need to be so formal, Beth"*.

Bethany says, *"I'm still shocked just to be in front of you"*. Daphne says, *"please don't treat me differently to Dawn; ok so, where we were with this toy boy?"*. Dawn rolls her eyes as Bethany says, *"Dawn might have feelings for Ralph."* Dawn tries to explain the situation calmly however Bethany and Dawn are not convinced. Eventually, Dawn takes a breath as she asks, *"who's ready to try on their outfit?"*. Bethany excitedly jumps up and down as she runs to the dressing room; Daphne asks, *"do you really like Ralph?"*. Dawn blushes as Daphne says, *"aww, look like Dawn has a crush".* Dawn says, *"I may like Ralph, but there's no way he will ever return my feelings...".* Daphne tries to reassure her as Dawn tries to change the subject just as Bethany returns wearing a red lace dress as Dawn says, *"wow, bestie you are slaying it!".* Dawn tells Daphne to get dressed next as Bethany feels nervous in her dress asking, *"are you sure it's perfect for the party?".* Dawn replies, *"of course, Beth you're rocking the dress".* Daphne soon comes out in a light pink pearly gown as Dawn and Bethany say, *"wow, Daphne! You look amazing".* Daphne thanks them as Bethany says, *"it's your turn, Dawn".* Dawn nervously asks, *"um... I need your help choosing".* Dawn heads to the dressing room as Bethany asks, *"Daphne what do you think about Ralph and Dawn? they could be a cute couple right...?".* Daphne nods replying, *"he's such a cool guy and honestly it's rare to find someone like him".* Dawn shows herself in three outfits to her friends as she eventually chooses a blue lace gown with silver sparkle. Daphne says, *"well, now that we are all dressed, we should head out".* Dawn says, *"give me a minute, girls, I have to use the bathroom".* Bethany smiles as Dawn saying, *"I am so excited, you'll get to experience this while visiting! I'll wait for you outside".* Dawn thanks her as Bethany and Daphne talk; Dawn takes a deep breath wondering, *'what have I got myself into? do I really want to become a princess? I guess I don't have a choice.. I hope things work out.'* As the girls come down; Dawn says nervously, *"this is so not my scene to be".* Daphne assures her, *"this is so much more fun than you could ever imagine".* Bethany says, *"as I said earlier, as long as there are hot boys and Princes to flirt with, I'm cool".* Ralph comes as Dawn says, *"oh, um... hi".* Ralph bows as Daphne says, *"hey Ralph".* Ralph smiles replying, *"hello, Princess Daphne".* Bethany waves as Ralph also waves back. Daphne asks, *"everything ok, Ralph?".* Ralph replies, *"yes, just the King wants to speak with Dawn".*

Daphne nods as she asks, *"Beth, let's go dance?".* Bethany asks, *"Dawn, will you be ok?".* Dawn nods replying, *"I'm good, go dance Beth".* Bethany and Daphne soon head inside as dawn asks Ralph, *"um... where is he?".* Ralph replies, *"he's in his study".* Dawn smiles taking a deep breath as Ralph says, *"you look stunning today"*. Dawn blushes as she thanks Ralph for the compliment saying, *"you don't look bad yourself."* Ralph asks, *"do you know where his study is, Princess?"*. Dawn shakes her head replying, *"I don't think so"*. Ralph says, *"I will take you, ok"*. Dawn smiles and thanks to him as they walk down the corridor as she asks nervously *"Ralph, do you think I will be good at being a princess?"*. Ralph looks at her for a second answering, *"I don't know, but I do know you're very gentle, sweet and this makes you a beautiful person, I believe you can do it"*. Dawn thanks him again as he soon opens a door as they enter Ralph bows as he says, *"Your Highness, I've brought Dawn here"*. Daniel says, *"thank you, Ralph. I would like you to head back to the party and keep an eye on things."* Ralph nods replying, *"as you wish, Your Highness"*. He turns to leave but not before saying, *"I'll see you shortly, Dawn"*. After Ralph leaves, Dawn looks at Daniel who asks, *"are you ready for this Princess?"*. Dawn replies, *"I am not sure, dad"*. Daniel assures her saying, *"Dawn, I believe you will do great"*.

Dawn asks worriedly, *"how can you be so sure?"*. Daniel replies, *"because you are your mother's child"*. Dawn gets a little emotional saying, *"I wish mom was here to see this"*. Daniel says sadly, *"me too, Princess.. but for now, it's just us and we can tell all about it once she's awake"*. Dawn smiles as Daniel say, *"onto a different topic, I have to introduce you to someone when we go out"*. Dawn asks, *"who?"*. Daniel replies, *"his name is Mason and he's a prince from a local country"*. Dawn looks shocked asking, *"are you trying to set me up?"*. Daniel laughs replying, *"no, Princess. I just want to introduce you to the other monarchies; I'd never force you to be with someone you didn't want to be with."* Dawn smiles as Daniel says, *"I think you will like him though"*. Dawn gives Daniel a hug as he says, *"I cannot wait to introduce you to everyone, you look beautiful Princess"*. Dawn smiles saying, *"thanks dad"*. Daniel nods saying, *"let's go introduce you as the new Princess"*. As they soon come out they see a guy in a royal outfit as Daniel says, *"well, hello there"*. He turns around as he bows, *"Your Highness"*. Daniel says, *"hello, Prince Mason"*.

Dawn looks at Mason as he asks, *"how are you this evening, Your Highness?"*. Daniel replies, *"it's a party, I am happy to have so many people here to celebrate though"*. Mason nods replying, *"I must admit there are many who do not understand the reason for this party"*. Daniel says, *"well, you won't have to worry any longer, I will be announcing it shortly"*. Mason nods as he sees Dawn looking at him as he says to Daniel, *"who is the beautiful lady beside you?"*. Daniel replies, *"this is Dawn, she's a special guest here tonight"*. Mason bows as he says, *"it's a pleasure to meet you"*. Dawn smiles saying, *"you too"*. Daniel and Dawn leave as they come outside the room he takes a deep breath as Daniel enters the party with everyone looking at him.

Chapter 11

Daniel says, *"good evening and welcomes to all, I am grateful for everyone's presence here tonight; I have brought you all together to make a very exciting announcement. As most of you are aware, my nephew Charlie is excepted to take the throne upon my death that is because I have not had a child of my own. However, not long ago, I was introduced to someone very important to me. she is here tonight, and I would like to explain that whilst this was a shock to me, it also made me celebrate too. I do not expect anyone to understand why the secret has been kept so long, but here it is. I am a father! I would like to welcome my daughter into my life and the royal family! Please welcome, Princess Dawn, the heir to the throne!".* Everyone looked at Dawn as she could feel the camera flashes in front of her; Daniel turns to Dawn asking, *"would you like to say anything, Princess?".* Dawn says, *"um.. excuse me I need air".* Dawn comes out into the balcony as she feels the air on her skin as she takes a deep breath when someone comes behind her saying, *"so, Princess Dawn, huh?".* Dawn turns to see Daphne as she nods; Daphne has a cold annoyed expression asking, *"why didn't you tell me, huh?".* Dawn says, *"are you mad at me because I didn't tell you?".* Daphne nods replying, *"why else should I not be mad at you?".* Dawn laughs as Daphne rolls her eyes and says, *"I wasn't sure I was who he thought me to be, I didn't want to say anything until I knew for sure."* Daphne nods replying, *"I guess that's fair, well welcome to the family! I have a female cousin! We are going to have to go shopping and do something about your hair thought...".* Just then Charlie comes in yelling, *"WHO THE HELL DO YOU THINK YOU ARE?".* Daphne turns to Charlie as she says, *"it's not polite to scream Charlie".* Charlie gives her a cold expression as she says, *"I wasn't talking you Daphne."* Dawn apologizes as Charlie says angrily, *"you came here to steal the crown from me, didn't you?".* Dawn was shocked by his words as he says, *"DON'T LIE TO ME!"*. Daphne tries to calm Charlie down as he says, *"I can't believe you're defending her!"*. Daphne nods answering, *"of course, I will defend her, she's family"*. Charlie laughs as he coldly says, *"she's not mine! family don't steal from each other!"*.

Charlie storms off as Daphne tries to assure Dawn who asks, *"Daphne can I tell you a secret?"*. Daphne excitedly replies, *"my first secret with my cousin! Yippee do tell!"*. Dawn takes a deep breath as she says, *"I don't want the crown or throne; I just wanted a relationship with my father. I just wanted to have my mother and father together at the same time so I could see what it's like to have both of my parents together. But it seems I am only able to have one at a time. And now, I'm being screamed for the one thing I didn't care about"*. Dawn begins to cry as Daphne apologizes and hugs her. Daniel comes over as he says, *"Daphne, can I have a moment alone with my daughter?"*. Daphne nods as she leaves; Dawn wipes her tears as she says sadly, *" Charlie doesn't like me."* Daniel asked, *"is it true what you just said?"*. Dawn nods as she replies, *"you mean that Charlie doesn't like me, yeah"*.

Daniel shakes his head asking, *"not that Dawn, you just want to have a relationship with me?"*. Dawn nervously replies, *"oh you heard that?"*. Daniel nods replying, *"yeah, I was worried about and came looking for you"*. Dawn nods as Daniel say, *"Dawn, I want that too. But now, you're also a princess; so, I want to be honest and forward with you; you're going to have to start learning how to be a monarch and soon you'll be taking lessons, meeting people and eventually you will need to find a husband so that when you can finally take over the crown from me- you are to be wed."* Dawn looks at her dad as she asks, *"you were never married, dad?"*. Daniel replies, *"I am different, I did not have to marry because I am a man."* Dawn's facial expression becomes angry as she says, *"excuse me? what do you mean by that?"*. Daniel replies, *"I mean, it's just how our monarchy works"*. Dawn looks at him angrily folding her arms and says, *"I am done with your lame party, I have a headache and will get some rest"*. Dawn walks away as Daniel tries to call her back. Soon in her room, Dawn breaks down as she says, *"I can't do this, there's so much to take in, and I... I just want my mom... I don't want to have this life... I just wish to be normal... I wish that stupid car accident never happened..."*. Her phone rings as Dawn answers, *"hello? oh my god! I am on my way!"*. Dawn runs out as she thinks, *"mom, I'm coming!"*.

Chapter 12

Dawn rushes over to the hospital as Bethany and Daphne soon arrive waiting in the corridor. Bethany says, *"I hope the news Dawn gets is good, I will be broken if anything happens to Amelia".* Daphne understood that Bethany was close to Dawn's mother; Bethany asks, *"Daphne, what will happen if something's wrong? I mean for Dawn".* Daphne replies, *"I don't know, but for sure Dawn will have no choice but to begin training immediately, which is boring but will take her mind off things".* Bethany looks concerned asking, *"will they allow her time to grieve for her loss?".* Daphne replies, *"her life is going change forever. I just hope we will still be able to have sleepovers".* Daphne laughs replying, *"I hope so too, but I have a feeling my uncle will be a little strict".* They both smiled for a second then remember Amelia; Bethany says, *"I will get us some hot chocolate".* Meanwhile, in the canteen, Daniel was feeling annoyed whilst Ralph tries to calm him down. Daniel asks, *"why can I not meet her?".* Ralph replies, *"sire, they have informed you, you are not family".* Daniel asks, *"how can I not be her family? she has my child".* Ralph says, *"yes sir, but that does not make you family".*

Daniel rolls his eyes as Ralph explains, *"sire, Dawn needs time alone with her mother, you need to give her the decision for the next step, alone".* Daniel nods as he takes a sip of herbal tea; Ralph asks, *"sire if you don't mind me asking, why are you so tensed over this?".* Daniel replies, *"Ralph, it's hard to explain".* Ralph gives him a sincere look with Daniel saying, *"I thought I had lost her, do you know what it's like loving someone? I still love Amelia with all my heart."* Ralph says, *"sire, I guessed it because it's obvious".* Daniel looks sad continuing, *"do you know how it feels to love someone, so much but never be able to get close to them, see them or hold them in your arms?".* Ralph takes a breath replying, *"sire... I do know that feeling, to have feelings for someone deeply and care so much but not be able to tell them."* Daniel asks, *"oh, Ralph is it anyone I know?"*.

Ralph shakes his head answering, *"It's better than me and she is not together."* Daniel wonders, *'who could be Ralph's love?'.* Back in the castle, Charlie was fuming and yells, *"HOW COULD THEY DO THIS TO ME?"*. Mason asks, *"aren't you being a little bit extreme now?"*. Charlie replies, *"for weeks, they lied to me and kept me in the dark. now the secret's exposed and they throw me aside like a piece of shit".* Mason tries to calm him down as Charlie asks, *"do you believe what is happening to be fair?"*. Mason replies, *"I don't agree but I think Dawn will be a great leader. she's cute".* Charlie rolls his eyes and angrily says, *"I've worked so hard my damn life for this! I am not going to let some low girl steal what is mine!".* Mason leaves whilst Charlie thinks, *'I need a plan to get rid of her and take back what belongs to me!'.* Back at the hospital, Dawn was in her mother's room crying when Amelia came over and embraced her. Amelia rubs her back saying, *"oh, my Princess, I'm fine".* Dawn says, *"I can't believe it, mom, I missed you so much".* Amelia says, *"I missed you too baby girl".* Dawn tells Amelia about Daniel and everything that happened recently. Amelia is surprised and stunned asking, *"how's he?".* Dawn replies, *"he's great, mom. why did you hide who I was and also my father?".* Amelia takes a deep breath replying, *"I never thought you'd meet him".* Dawn gives her mom a glare saying, *"say his name mom".* Amelia is reluctant however finally replies, *"King Daniel".* Dawn snaps at her mom telling her, *"Do you know what you did for the past sixteen years? you lied to me and him, you took his chance of becoming a dad."* Amelia sadly says, *"I had no choice; it was for your own protection Dawn from his mother".* dawn says, *"I have never met the woman mom."* Amelia tells her, *"You have no clue what the woman can do. you may hate me Dawn, but the truth is I loved your father and still do, when I found out about you I wanted to tell him, but his mom was filled with hatred towards me... if I told him then he would have told his mom... this is the reason why I kept it all a secret from you."* Amelia cries as Dawn hugs her mom saying, *"I don't blame or hate you mom".* Dawn asks, *"mom, have you seen dad since that day?"*. Amelia replies, *"no, but I know what you're thinking, and I don't want to see him tonight... I'm tired and I want to spend the night with my daughter".* Dawn smiles, *"of course mom, I will head out to let everyone know you're ok and then I'll get some food".* Amelia says, *"my favorite which is..."* Amelia and Dawn both say, *"Chinese".*

They laugh as Dawn comes out to see everyone waiting. Bethany and Daniel both ask, *"Dawn, what's going on? how's Amelia?".* Dawn replies, *"mom's better but tired".* Bethany breaks down happily with Daphne who hugs her. Daniel asks, *"may I meet her?".* Dawn replies, *"no dad, sorry. mom is very tired and doesn't want to see anyone right now".* Daniel understands sadly; Daphne and Bethany head out whilst Ralph bows to Dawn saying, *"I am so happy for you, Princess".* Dawn giggles replying, *"Ralph, I've told you don't address me as such. you're my friend..".* Ralph tries to justify his position, but Daniel says, *"whatever Dawn wants, you must follow".* Ralph apologizes as Dawn kisses his cheek telling him, *"Thanks a lot Ralph, you've been so wonderful, and I don't think I would have made it this far without you".* Ralph is stunned replying nervously, *"yeah... sure.. of course.. I will... give you space".* Daniel finds Ralph behaving weirdly and comes closer to Dawn asking, *"let me guess, I also have to leave".* Dawn apologizes to Daniel who looks sadly at her. Dawn hugs her dad saying, *"me and mom will see you in the morning".* Daniel asks surprised, *"you're spending the night here?".* Dawn nods, *"yep, I missed mom a lot and need to catch up. is that ok with you?".* Daniel nods and says, *"just pass the message that I am happy she's ok".* Daniel leaves as Dawn heads to the canteen and brings Chinese food. She comes back to her mom's room with the food. However, Amelia is fast asleep, Dawn says, *"just one more night mom, then you will meet dad".*

Chapter 13

The next morning, Dawn comes to her mom's room holding two lattes. She doesn't see her mom around and asks, *"mom? where are you?"*. Amelia comes out from the bathroom replying, *"I'm here sweetie"*. Dawn says, *"mom, we are going to see dad! you can't wear your hospital gown"*. Amelia asks, *"does it matter Princess?"*. Dawn folds her arm replying, *"you are NOT going dressed in that"*. Amelia laughs as Dawn heads outside for a minute and comes back holding a causal dress. Amelia heads back to the bathroom to change whilst Dawn drinks her latte. Amelia looks at herself in the mirror wondering, *'am I really ready to face him after all this time?'*. Outside, awn calls Daniel and tells him, *"mom and I will meet you in the garden"*. Dawn shouts, *"mom hurry up, dad's waiting for us in the garden"*. Amelia comes out as Dawn says, *"mom, you look beautiful"*. Amelia smiles saying, *"you've always had the best fashion sense"*. Dawn says, *"come on mom."* Amelia grabs her latte before heading out. Meanwhile, Daniel was waiting in the garden however felt nervous thinking, *'I can do this, I can do this.'* Dawn arrives and surprises her dad who says, *"hey Dawn"*.

Amelia and Daniel look and wave to each other. Dawn notices the awkwardness between them and says, *"I'm going to get some snack and maybe take a walk, have a good chat"*. She leaves her parents alone; Daniel smiles saying, *"Amy, you still look gorgeous"*. Amelia blushes and thanks Daniel. Daniel says nervously, *"I guess we have a few things to address like the elephant in the room"*. Amelia nods, Daniel asks, *"why didn't you tell me about Dawn?"*. Amelia replies, *"because of your mom"*. Daniel asks stunned, *"what about my mom?"*. Amelia answers, *"you know, she frightens me."* Daniel says, *"I wouldn't have allowed her to do anything"*. Amelia takes a deep breath saying, *"Danny, we both know that's not true, what happened years ago between us... I mean we didn't end on good terms".* Daniel looks sadly at her asking, *"Were you ever planning on telling me?".* Amelia replies, *"the day we broke up, I wanted to tell you, but you were so adamant on speaking first".* Daniel says, *"I would have known then".* Amelia nods apologizing, *"I'm sorry I never told you, I was afraid...".* Amelia starts to cry just as Daniel hugs her saying, *"I understand your feelings, but it still hurts".* Meanwhile, Dawn was in the canteen eating a croissant when Ralph came behind Dawn. Dawn turns and was about to fall when Ralph caught her. They shared an eyelock as he helped her up. Dawn says, *"Ralph! you frightened me!".* Ralph says, *"I'm sorry, Princess".* Dawn gives him a cold glare, Ralph says, *"I mean, Dawn".* She smiles and thanks to him. Ralph asks, *"where's your mom?".* Dawn replies, *"she's talking with dad in the garden".* Ralph asks, *"how are you feeling?".* Dawn replies, *"I'm really happy".* Ralph smiles at her saying, *"that's a good thing then".* Dawn turns back to her pastries asking, *"would you like one, Ralph?".* Ralph nods and takes one. Dawn says, *"I think love is the key to life, mom and dad may have a second chance."* Ralph smiles saying, *"I'm pleased, do you... er....um... love or have feelings for anyone?".* Dawn shakes her head replying, *"not at the moment".* Ralph looked sad as Dawn resumed, *"I've been so overwhelmed with everything lately, I haven't had time to focus on guys".* Ralph asks, *"Dawn I'm going to grab a coffee, would you like one?".* Dawn replies, *"no thanks, I have my latte".* Ralph goes in the opposite direction leaving Dawn to wonder, *'what's up with Ralph?".* Dawn grabs another croissant to eat when a voice startles her from the back. Dawn turns to see Mason; she asks, *"why is everyone frightening me today?".*

Mason apologises as Dawn says, *"it's Mason right?".* Mason says, *"I don't think we've properly introduced".* He bows saying, *"I'm Prince Mason".* Mason gives Dawn some tips on introductions when meeting another royal person. Dawn curtsies and says, *"nice to meet you, I'm Princess Dawn".* Mason asks, *"how are you feeling about everything that has happened lately?".* Dawn replies, *"a mix of emotions, happy, excited, nervous".* Mason smiles and assures her that everything will be fine.

Dawn says, *"thanks for your kind words Prince Mason"*. Mason says, *"you can call me Mason as we are both royalty"*. Dawn smiles and nods. Mason tries to flirt with Dawn just as Ralph comes back with a jealous expression. Dawn says, *"hey Ralph, it's good you are back"*. Ralph bows and says, *"Prince Mason, Princess Dawn"*. Mason says, *"pleasure to see you again, Raphael, I must head back to the castle"*. Dawn waves goodbye to Mason who leaves. Ralph asks, *"are you alright, Dawn?"*. Dawn replies, *"of course, Ralph. why are you asking me this?"*. Ralph answers, *"well.. um... you see Prince Mason has kind of a reputation"*. Dawn says, *"what kind?"*. Ralph is nervous but says, *"it's not my place to say anything.. he's what one would call a 'player' or 'womanizer'. he's not a faithful partner."* Dawn laughs and says, *"he's an interesting person, someone I would like to get to know more about but he's for sure not the type of guy I would go for"*. Ralph feels reassured to hear this and thinks, *'why am I feeling so much happiness right now?'*. Before Ralph can ask another question, Dawn's phone rings. Dawn soon ends the call telling, *"Ralph, my parents are calling me"*. Ralph says, *"I will see you back at the castle, Dawn"*. Dawn waves bye as Ralph watches her go. Dawn comes back to the garden and feels the tension in the air. She asks, *"what's going on?"*. Daniel says, *"I am telling your mom to come back to the castle and continue her treatment"*. Amelia firmly declines and says, *"I would rather go home than go with you"*. Dawn is stunned by her mom's response asking, *"why won't you with dad and me?"*. Amelia looks at Daniel asking, *"do you want to tell her, or should I?"*. Daniel tries to explain however Amelia says, *"his mother, your grandmother, the Queen is at the castle."* Daniel says to Dawn, *"she wants to see you, sweetie"*. Dawn didn't know what to say and looked at her parents.

Chapter 14

Dawn looks at her dad with a shocked expression saying, *"oh dear!"*. Amelia says, *"that's what I just said, Princess"*. Daniel says, *"she's not that bad"*. Amelia rolls her eyes saying, *"don't even get me started!"*. Dawn nervously asks, *"er... do I have to meet her?"*. Daniel nods while Dawn says, *"dad, when do I...?"*. Amelia replies angrily, *"when I say so"*. Daniel tries to calm her down saying, *"you and me both know that's not going to work, she's very adamant and whatever she demands, she gets"*. Dawn felt super worried and nervous while Amelia says, *"if Dawn is to meet the queen, I will be by Dawn's side"*. Daniel shook his head saying, *"no, I give you my word that I will be there, and I won't let anything bad happen"*. Amelia screams, *"I WILL BE IN THE ROOM WITH DAWN, AND THAT'S FINAL!"*. Dawn says, *"dad, you are not going to win"*. Daniel finally agrees and says, *"I will prove that I will be by both of your sides, no matter what, ok?"*. Amelia blushes as Dawn says, *"you two are so cute"*. Dawn asks, *"do I have a say in this matter?"*. Daniel replies, *"unfortunately no, your grandmother is a very strong woman, she gets what she wants"*. Amelia says, *"except for my daughter."* Daniel promises, *"I will make sure she doesn't get to Dawn, but I have to meet her and calm her down"*. Daniel's phone rings and he soon leaves. Amelia was about to leave when Dawn called her back. Amelia asks, *"what's the matter, Princess?"*. Dawn replies, *"mom, I'm feeling scared and worried... I know it's not important... but I feel embarrassed about you know..."*. Amelia hugs Dawn and strokes her back lovingly. Dawn asks, *"is it too late to run away and hide?"*. Amelia laughs replying, *"I wish we could do that, but no Dawn, we need to see her"*. Dawn asks, *"mom, what if she doesn't like me?"*. Amelia replies, *"she probably won't. it's who she is"*. Dawn rolls her eyes and says, *"I really hope you're wrong"*. Amelia says, *"I doubt it"*. Bethany comes and says, *"Amelia"*.

Amelia hugs Bethany warmly who cries happily. Amelia says, *"I missed you dearly, how have you been?"*. Bethany cries replying, *"I'm ok"*. Amelia asks, *"how about me and you have a catchup? would you like to go back to my room and watch movies and have snacks?"*. Bethany nods and runs excitedly. Amelia says, *"come on Princess, let's head back for now and have fun"*. Dawn nods and they soon head back into the hospital. Elsewhere, Daniel was in the study when a voice says, *"do not tell me what I hear is true"*. Daniel asks, *"what are you talking about mom?"*. Queen Matilda says, *"do not play dumb with me, Daniel."* Daniel says, *"sorry, I need you to be more specific"*. Queen Matilda angrily asks, *"did you father a child out of marriage?"*. Daniel replies, *"oh, well yeah, I guess I did"*. Queen Matilda is not pleased with all and says, *"Daniel, I cannot believe you did this to us"*. Daniel says, *"mom, I didn't know until just recently"*. She angrily says, *"I don't care when you found out you had a bastard child, you had one!"*. Daniel says, *"mother, I ask that you call her Dawn. that is her name"*. Queen Matilda says, *"I do not care whatever is her name! who is the child's mother?"*. Daniel tries to beat around the bush however she yells, *"TELL ME NOW!"*. Daniel says, *"Amelia"*. Queen Matilda rolls her eyes saying, *"of course, it was that girl"*. Daniel snaps saying, *"do not speak of her in that way."* She asks, *"have you done a paternity test to prove this girl's claim?"*. Daniel answers, *"yes, mother. and she is definitely my child"*. The Queen says, *"you just couldn't keep it in your pants, could you?"*. Daniel says, *"I am not even going to reply to that comment. Dawn is my daughter and your granddaughter"*. Ralph comes in and bows; the Queen angrily says, *"what do you want, Ralph?"*. Ralph replies, *"I just have a quick message for the King."* The Queen looks at him and tells, *"speak without hesitation in front of both of us, please!"*. Ralph says, *"I apologize however I was told this should be just for him"*. Queen Matilda glares at Ralph who takes a deep breath and says, *"sire, I wanted to let you know that Amelia will be discharged from the hospital tomorrow. Dawn will be spending the night with her mother in the hospital."* Daniel smiles and says, *"wonderful news, thank you, Ralph"*.

Ralph bows and leaves as Queen Matilda asks, *"hold on Daniel! why does it matter when she is being discharged?"*. Daniel replies, *"um... well... I haven't mentioned it yet. I have Dawn and Amelia coming to live here whilst Amelia continues her recovery from the accident."* Queen Matilda angrily says, *"you've got to be kidding me!"*. Daniel shakes his head and yawns saying, *"it's late mom, I'm tired and I will speak to you in the morning"*. The Queen says, *"don't you dare walk away!"*. Daniel turns, wishes his mom goodnight and leaves. The next day, Amelia changes and says, *"Dawn, hurry up please"*. Dawn says, *"sorry mom, I just don't know what to wear"*. Amelia says, *"a dress would be nice"*. Dawn says, *"mom, please help me instead of making fun of me!"*. Dawn eventually comes out in a dark blue dress as Amelia asks, *"are you ready to meet the Queen?"*. Dawn replies, *"yeah but um... what do I even call her?"*. Amelia says, *"Her Majesty? I don't see her as being the 'grandma' type."'* Dawn nods and takes a deep breath while Amelia heads out. Dawn thinks, *'I hope everything goes well.'*

Chapter 15

In the living room, Queen Matilda and King Daniel were both waiting. Queen Matilda says, *"I hope they actually show up"*. Daniel says, *"mom, they will. they are inside the castle"*. Amelia soon enters, curtsies, and says, *"hello, your Majesty"*. Queen Matilda rolls her eyes replying, *"don't play with me, where is the girl?"*. Amelia says, *"I wanted to come in first and speak with you myself. I need to know what you are planning with her before I let her anywhere near you"*. Queen Matilda says angrily, *"how dare you?"*. Daniel defends Amelia saying, *"mom, she has a clear point. she's a mom herself and it's only natural for her to worry"*. Amelia smiles and thanks to Daniel; Queen Matilda says, *"please, bring the girl in"*. Amelia says, *"you haven't answered my question"*. Queen Matilda replies, *"she will be trained and taught into her new role as the crowned Princess. is that all you need?"*. Amelia says, *"nearly, do you promise as her grandmother to protect her?"*. Queen Matilda replies, *"of course."* Amelia says, *"that's all I wanted to know"*. Amelia calls Dawn inside who looks nervously at Queen Matilda. She curtsies and greets, *"hi"*. Queen Matilda says, *"hi to you too young lady."* Dawn smiles and says, *"it's a pleasure to meet you"*.

Queen Matilda says sarcastically, *"I wish the feeling was mutual"*. Daniel says *"mom"*. Queen Matilda says, *"it's a pleasure to meet you too. well, Daniel, I can't say I am overjoyed at you being unable to keep it in your pants-however at least she's a beautiful girl and will be able to marry her off quickly."* Daniel says, *"mom! that is disgusting"*. Dawn and Amelia were both annoyed and shocked; Dawn asks, *"do I have a say in this?"*. Queen Matilda says, *"I mean, I am not pleased that my son got a commoner pregnant however this young lady looks a lot like me, so we have that going for us"*. Daniel says, *"mom, now is the time to stop!"*. Dawn says, *"really, you are going to leave me hanging?"*. Daniel

46

says, *"hold on a sec, dawn"*. Queen Matilda says, *"well, we'd probably be starting her training soon too, shouldn't we?"*. Dawn says, *"enough, I'm sorry but I want to say something"*. Queen Matilda says, *"until you are trained to be a proper Princess, you may not speak unless spoken to. am I clear?"*. Dawn replies angrily, *"no, no it's not clear!"*. Queen Matilda sternly says, *"your opinion doesn't matter! be quiet!"*. Daniel says, *"Dawn, we will discuss things later"*. Amelia steps in saying, *"no, you won't I will"*. Dawn screams, *"AAAAAAAH! I can't take this anymore!"*. She runs out, Amelia says, *"I will handle this as for your mom she should be ashamed of herself. do you know Dawn was scared to meet you in case you would react like this? like it or not she's your granddaughter and now she will never trust you enough to listen to you"*. Amelia heads out while Daniel turns to his mom who says, *"Daniel, I don't think she has what it takes to be a Princess"*. Daniel says frustrated, *"mom, I can't believe you! you are going to chase away my child and the love of my life in one second"*. Queen Matilda is shocked and stunned by his words as he says, *"if you do, I will never forgive you!"*. Daniel leaves the room while her expression looks remorseful. Elsewhere, Dawn is in her room crying and screaming, *"I can't do this anymore!"*. Amelia enters and Dawn turns to ask, *"what do you want mom?"*. Amelia says, *"I am sorry sweetie for the way she treated you."* Dawn asks, *"how could she speak to me like that? like I was a piece of trash? has she ignored the fact I am her granddaughter?"*. Amelia tries to calm things down. Dawn takes a deep breath and says, *"mom, I want to be alone right now"*. Amelia understands and leaves the room; Dawn thinks about everything when suddenly Daphne comes in. She says, *"hey cuz, is this a bad time?"*. Dawn turns to face her and tells her what happened in the living room.

Daphne apologizes; however, Dawn says, *"you are not to blame! do you think the Queen will ever accept me?"*. Daphne tries to assure Dawn who cries wishing, *"I wish my dad was normal and life wasn't so complicated"*. Daphne says, *"I believe in you, and I know you will be a great Princess"*. Dawn asks, *"Daph, can I have a few moments alone? I am feeling tired"*. Daphne leaves while Dawn heads to the closet and changes into something comfy. She soon comes back inside her room when Ralph says, *"Dawn? can I come in?"*. Dawn says, *"sure, Ralph"*. Ralph enters and says, *"I heard about your meeting with the Queen, how are you feeling?"*. Dawn replies sadly, *"expected something like that to happen because If you expect disappointment, then you can never really be disappointed"*. Ralph says, *"I know she can be too much.."*. Ralph notices Dawn upset asking, *"how would you like to get some fresh air and take a walk in the garden?"*. Dawn replies, *"ok."* They soon head outside however Dawn begins to feel emotional and cries; Ralph says, *"oh no, Dawn is you ok?"*. Dawn replies sadly, *"this is so overwhelming, Ralph"*. Ralph hugs her and says, *"Dawn, it's ok, I'm here for your promise. I promise to never leave your side, I promise to be your friend no matter what."* Dawn says, *"thanks Ralph, what would I do without you? but why, are you so nice to me?"*. Ralph says, *"I love you, Dawn"*. Dawn breaks the hug and looks at him shocked. Ralph says, *"um... I mean.. not love-love but love as in you have become one of my closest dearest friends... it's not what I meant Dawn.."* Ralph thinks, *'damn, I'm an idiot.'* Dawn says, *"you said, you loved me..."*. Ralph takes a breath and says, *"yeah, like a friend, I explained that"*. Dawn says, *"I don't believe it's just friendly. you are lying to me now and I know you have feelings for me as the crowned Princess I insist you tell me the truth"*. Ralph says, *"look, I didn't mean it the way it came across, I know you have a lot to think about; I don't think anything past being your friend and just want to be there for you"*. Dawn says, *"you do love me!"*. Ralph tries to calm her down however she cries saying, *"oh! come on, first I thought I would lose my mom, I meet my dad for the very first time, I find out I am a Princess and my life changes, I get my mom back, I meet the Queen who despises me and now the only person I trusted to be there for me tells me he loves me. I can't deal with all this right now!"*. Dawn runs off as Ralph looks sadly thinking, *'I've screwed up.'*

Chapter 16

Two weeks passed, and Dawn was in her room thinking, *'I can't believe it's been two weeks since I last spoke with Ralph... I still can't believe he said he loved me.. did I overreact?.. I'd better get ready.'* Dawn comes to the closet and chose a blue and turquoise maxi dress; there is a knock on the door while Dawn does her hair, Daphne enters asking, *"are you ready, cuz?"*. Dawn nods and they leave; Daphne says, *"you will love being a Princess, it's fun!"*. Dawn opens the study to see Queen Matilda who begins their lesson. A few hours later after training, Dawn comes to the garden for some fresh air when suddenly someone comes behind her. Dawn turns to see Prince Mason, she says, *"Mason, you scared me!"*. Mason bows and apologizes before asking, *"how do you feel after your lessons, Dawn?"*. Dawn replies, *"my brain feels like a sponge trying to absorb all the data"*. Mason says, *"it's a lot to learn, what you need is a tutor"*. Dawn asks, *"any suggestions where I may find one?"*. Mason asks, *"how about me?"*. Dawn is a little reluctant and replies, *"would you be committing it?"*. He nods saying, *"sure, I'd love to"*. Dawn teases Mason who says, *"we can also use this as an opportunity to get to know more about each other"*. Dawn nods nervously and he soon leaves. Dawn is left in thought and is also unaware that Charlie had been spying on her. Charlie thinks, *'hmm... I think I have an idea how to get rid of her.. but first I will hurt her...'*. He comes inside and sees Bethany who bows to him. Bethany waves, *"hi"* and he replies, *"hi, you must be Bethany right?"*. Bethany nods replying, *"you can call me Beth"*. Charlie asks, *"how do you know my dear cousin?"*. Bethany replies, *"we've been friends since pre-school, and we are like sisters"*. Charlie says, *"aww, that's lovely.. were you always the sweeter one?"*.

Bethany feels a little embarrassed and nervous saying, *"um...er.."*. Charlie continues to compliment Bethany who blushes and says, *"I'm not usually, the one that is considered gorgeous, but it's nice to hear it from you".* Charlie says, *"you are fabulous and the most attractive girl I have ever met. never doubt yourself.. I bet Dawn steals all the attention".* Bethany says, *"um, yeah I guess she does, I mean it doesn't make a difference to me".* Charlie says, *"it matters to me that no one can see your true beauty next to that cousin of mine".* Bethany says, *"I mean, Dawn is cuter than me".* Charlie comes closer saying, *"I don't want to hear you say that again... I want to hear you call yourself sexy and stunning, Beth".* Beth says, *"I am sexy".* Bethany says, *"I appreciate this pep talk- but I am not sure why you are doing this".* Charlie says, *"I want to take you out if you give me a chance".* Bethany was stunned asking, *"what?".* Charlie flirts with her and comes closer; Bethany blushes while Charlie kisses her warmly. Dawn comes in stunned to see them asking, *"Beth? what's going on?".* Charlie says, *"Beth babe, I look forward to our date."* Charlie leaves while Dawn looks at Bethany who says, *"hey girl, it's not what you think...".* Dawn says, *"your happiness is my happiness... I hope you enjoy your date with Charlie."* Bethany apologizes however Dawn says, *"I need to go and practice my training lessons."* Bethany asks, *"why are you so bothered and upset about this?".* Dawn turns to Bethany replying, *"Beth, we tell each other everything... and now that I am becoming a Princess it's like you forget to tell me things like dating a Prince".* Bethany says, *"that's not fair, Dawn!".* Dawn angrily says, *"not fair? I'll tell you what's not fair, I now have to learn how to be a Princess! I've had everything taken away from me! I am losing myself here to become something I never wanted!".* Bethany says, *"stop it! I haven't done anything if you just let me talk".* Dawn screams, *"NO! I want to be alone, and don't bother talking to me now!".* Dawn heads to her room and cries wondering, *'am I to blame? I can't believe I said all that to Beth...I should go apologies later.'* Just then, Daphne enters the room and sees Dawn who tells her about the argument with Bethany. Daphne is surprised when Dawn tells her about Bethany and Charlie dating. Daphne asks, *"are you sure? because my brother's true love is the crown!".* Dawn asks, *"why is he after Beth anyway?".* Daphne replies, *"who knows? but I am highly suspicious of him".* Daphne says, *"I came here to see if you need any help with your training?".* Dawn replies, *"I am actually working with someone else to help me... Prince Mason has offered to be my tutor."* Daphne was surprised and says, *"ok, just keep an eye on Mason he has a past of being a womanizer and player".* Dawn nods while Daphne agrees to help with other training mainly girly aspects. Dawn says, *"thanks, hope no boy drama?".* Daphne asks, *"how are things between you and Ralph?".* Dawn replies, *"actually, I haven't spoken to him these last two weeks...".* Daphne was surprised especially when Dawn told her, *"he said, he loved me".* Daphne was supportive however Dawn says, *"I am in no position be dating or even be in a relationship with someone right now. I need to handle my own life."* Daphne says, *"I ship you two... Dawn or dalph?".*

Dawn rolls her eyes while Daphne gave her some emotional advice about her feelings. Dawn thought, *'maybe she's right, perhaps I need to open up to the idea of loving someone...'.* Just then Ralph came in and bowed saying, *"Princesses.. I was sent to see if Dawn was available to meet with the Queen".* Daphne excuses herself and leaves. Ralph says, *"I'd better leave too Princess".* Dawn says, *"wait, hold on Ralph?".* Ralph stops and turns back; Dawn says, *"I'm really sorry how I reacted the other day Ralph, can I tell you something? I'm afraid and have a lot going on right now...".* Ralph is understanding while Dawn says, *"I'm open to the idea of dating someone as long as they take things slow with me and work with me while I adjust to this new life."* Ralph takes a deep breath asking, *"are you saying you may be interested in me?".* Dawn nods replying, *"possibly? but can we take things very slow and leave other options open?".* Ralph smiles and nods saying, *"sure, I'm fine with this."* Dawn thanks him and kisses his cheek; He blushes and asks, *"what was that for?".* Dawn smiles, *"I appreciate, and I am thankful for you Ralph".* She leaves while Ralph thinks, *'me too, princess, I love you too'.*

Chapter 17

Dawn comes to the garden to meet Queen Matilda. She curtsies asking, *"you called for me, Your Majesty?"*. Queen Matilda says, *"I see you are learning some manners"*. Dawn replies, *"yes, I am trying to, I promise"*. Queen Matilda says, *"well, you seem to be understanding and learning well. I wanted to speak to you for a moment"*. Dawn nods as Queen Matilda say, *"I wanted to get to know you, as my granddaughter, I would like to know you better."* Dawn was surprised asking, *"really?"*. Queen Matilda says, *"don't look too surprised, my dear, it was bound to happen eventually. I need to make sure you are the right one to take over the throne"*. Dawn looks sadly saying, *"oh, right"*. Queen Matilda asks, *"why don't you start by telling me a bit about yourself? your life, and everything?"*. Dawn smiles and tells Queen Matilda about her childhood and how Amelia raised her with love and care especially the nickname *'Princess'*. After hearing the story, Queen Matilda says, *"it appears you had a wonderful life"*. Dawn smiles and replies, *"I most definitely have, this has been a huge adjustment though for me.. finding out I'm a Princess"*. Queen Matilda says, *"I can imagine, I wanted to apologize my dear for earlier, my world got turned upside down when I found out about you. I want to build a relationship with you- as my beloved granddaughter. will you accept my apology?"*. Dawn takes a deep breath saying, *"well... I am certainly willing to accept"*. Queen Matilda smiles and says, *"oh, I am so pleased"*. Dawn says, *"I want to make sure I have a relationship with my only grandparent"*.

Queen Matilda was stunned asking, *"what do you mean by, 'only grandparent'?"*. Dawn replies, *"well I don't have any family other than my mom. I mean not until you and dad came into the picture."* Queen Matilda asks, *"if you don't mind me asking, what happened to your other grandparents? you know your mother's family?"*. Dawn replies, *"I've never* met them, and mom has said that she isn't sure herself". Queen Matilda asks, "she isn't sure what happened to her own family?". Dawn says, "I think mom told me that she doesn't remember her family, but I have no idea, I've never met or knew them so I assume they could be alive for all we know". Queen Matilda says, "well, my dear- we are here now, and we will always take care of you as our family". Dawn thanks her. Queen Matilda asks, "may I ask you a question, dear?". Dawn replies, "sure, yes, of course". Queen Matilda asks, "what do you think of Prince Mason?". Dawn asks, "excuse me?". Queen Matilda says, "I have been told many things about him and I am curious as to your observations of him?". Dawn says, "oh. Um... he seems nice enough. he has offered to help me with my lessons". Queen Matilda says, "and? have you decided to work with him?". Dawn nods, "yes, I have. I want to make an impression and I need the help". Queen Matilda, "I am glad to hear that you are taking this entire situation very seriously." Dawn smiles and Queen Matilda say, "I will be honest and forward, my dear. as our Princess, you will be expected to find someone and marry by the age of twenty-one." Dawn says, "what? by 21 but I'm only 16 now...". Queen Matilda says, "that means, five years for us to find you a spouse". Dawn says, "but I don't know if I want to marry someone I barely feel anything for". Queen Matilda says, "I did, and I got two incredible children from it". Dawn says, "but that's not me... I want to get to know someone and love them; I am still just a teenager learning what I want in life". Queen Matilda says, "my dear- in most people's eyes, marrying a Prince is the proper plan for a Princess." Dawn asks, "but why must I marry, or even consider marrying, a Prince? can I not just marry someone who is of my choosing? someone I love?".

Queen Matilda rolls her eyes and says, "love. my dear, as wonderful as it would be to fall in love, it is vital for us to keep our bloodlines growing strong. not something you would understand but that is a completely different matter". Dawn says, "I was born into royalty but that means I am not of the pure bloodline". Queen Matilda says, "correct, which is why it is vital to fix this for future generations. at least take a chance and get to know Mason. would you be ok with that?". Dawn replies, "I guess so". Queen Matilda says, "you never know, you may find you really care for the young man". Dawn says, "maybe". Queen Matilda asks, "now, when are you speaking to him again?". Dawn replies, "tomorrow afternoon". Queen Matilda says, "I would like for you to report back to me what you think of him, I trust your judgment on whether he is a good man or not, plus it will give you a chance to see if he has the potential to be a good husband". Dawn thought, 'seriously?'. Queen Matilda asks, "what is your reply dear?". Dawn answers, "I am happy to take the time to get to know Prince Mason, I will report to you of any thought and feelings which I may have towards him. I will gladly consider him as a possible husband."

Queen Matilda is pleased with Dawn's answer and takes leaves. Dawn sadly thinks, 'what have I just consented to?'. Unaware Ralph has seen the whole conversation and sadly thinks, 'didn't Dawn just tell me she was interested in me? why is she thinking of Prince Mason? why does she say she cares, knowing how I feel, only to turn around and agree to entertain him too?'. Dawn turns to leave and sees Ralph who says, "hey, Dawn". Dawn says, "hi... how... how are you?". Ralph replies, "great, I feel good". Dawn thinks, 'I hope he didn't hear much'. Dawn asks, "how long have you been here?". Ralph replies, "not long, I just came here". Dawn smiles at Ralph who asks, "would you like to go on a walk?". Dawn replies, "sure, that sounds wonderful, Ralph. I need some time to not be thinking about being a Princess and all that comes with it". Ralph says, "let's head around the garden and we can get to know each other better". Dawn nods and begins to walk while Ralph thinks, 'I really hope that I'm not falling for someone that will never happen'. Dawn giggles asking, "Ralph, are you coming?." Ralph replies, "absolutely Princess". He then heads off to follow Dawn.

Chapter 18

The next morning, Dawn had training with Mason. She came into the living room, bowed in greeting, and said, *"hi Mason"*. Mason bowed and replied, *"hello, Dawn"*. Mason says, *"you should curtsey when you greet someone, not bow"*. Dawn smiles and says, *"ok, I've got that!"*. Dawn asks, *"so, what is our lesson today?"*. Mason replies, *"language"*. Dawn was confused asking, *"language?"*. Mason says, *"yes, language. you know how to speak to someone"*. Dawn says annoyed, *"excuse me? I know how to speak to people"*. She rolls her eyes while Mason says, *"obviously not; as a Princess, you are not allowed to roll your eyes, nor must you make comments about things with a snarky attitude atleast not in public. behind closed doors with your husband is a different story...now, we must learn proper speech, so you know how to handle all kinds of situations."* Dawn nods looking at Mason who gives her a scenario, *"let's say someone comes to you and tells you they believe their husband is cheating. how would you respond?"*. Dawn rolls her eyes and says, *"tell them to go speak to their husband and find out"*. Mason says, *"you've failed at this"*. Dawn asks, *"and why is that?"*. Mason replies, *"you rolled your eyes"*. Dawn says, *"oh...yeah... I did, didn't I?"*. Mason nods while Dawn asks, *"how do you... Do you know stop that?"*. Mason replies, *"be aware of yourself and practice, that's kind of the only way."* Dawn nods as Mason says, *"don't worry though, we will keep practicing until you get it right."* Dawn smiles and says, *"sounds great"*. Mason says, *"I could hear the sarcasm, but no eyeroll. good progress already, now we can work on one other important aspect of speech."* Dawn says, *"I've got this, what is it?"*. Mason replies, *"speaking to a suitor"*.

Dawn felt nervous while Mason says, *"so, when a possible suitor asks you out on a date, it is best if you give them a chance."* Dawn asks, *"what if I don't want to give them a chance?"*. Mason replies, *"that's your decision, but you should politely decline".* Dawn nods and Mason asks, *"let's have a practice shall we?".* Mason bows saying, *"Princess Dawn, I would very much like to take you out on a date tonight."* Dawn replies, *"no, thank you".* Mason rolls his eyes while Dawn says, *"you shouldn't roll your eyes, it's not ok for a royal."* She laughs while Mason says, *"you think that's funny?".* Dawn says, *"very much so, yes".* Mason asks, *"what do you seriously think about me taking you out on a date tonight?".* Dawn was stunned replying, *"excuse me?".* Mason says, *"I would like to take you out, if you would like to, that is".* Dawn says, *"oh... um...".* Mason asks for a chance while Dawn thinks, *'oh god, should I give him this chance? I know what grandma wants me to do... but do I see him that way?... could I see him that way?'.* Mason says, *"Dawn?".* Dawn snaps out of her thoughts saying, *"um...sorry...sure".* Mason says, *"sure?".* Dawn says, *"of course, yeah...sure".* Mason was confused asking, *"I'm not sure, Princess, what you intend by that response, can you be a little clearer?".* Dawn says, *"yes, I will go out with you".* Mason smiles and says, *"then I think we have done enough for today, go to your room and get ready".* Dawn asks, *"why?".* Mason replies, *"I am taking you out on a date tonight. I will pick you up at 7PM".* Dawn says, *"oh..ok".* He bows and leaves. Dawn thinks, *'I'd better find Daphne'.* Later on, that afternoon, Daphne came to see Dawn in her room. Daphne says, *"um... I've brought someone along".* Dawn asks, *"who?".* Bethany comes in and says, *"hey Dawn".* Dawn says surprised, *"oh, hey".* Daphne says, *"I think you two need to sort things out, I'll be waiting outside".* Bethany says, *"Dawn, please-".* Dawn says, *"no, Beth, I'm sorry. if my cousin makes you happy, then I'm happy for you. well, I can't say I'm happy, but I'll get used to it I guess".* Bethany laughs asking, *"you actually think I like him?".* Dawn asks, *"don't you?".* Bethany laughs replying, *"no! of course not, I don't like him at all."* Dawn asks, *"then why did I see you guys kissing?".* Bethany replies, *"he kissed me, I was just speaking to him, and he planted one on me, I was caught off guard just as you".* Dawn says, *"well... that's a bit awkward...".* They both laugh just as Daphne comes in asking, *"does the laughter mean you both sorted things and are back to normal?".* Dawn says, *"definitely, I could never stay mad at Beth. in fact, I don't even think I was mad. I think it was more in shock."* Bethany says, *"me too, but I know my bestie will always come back to me- even if we do fight".*

Bethany and Dawn share a hug. Dawn says, *"I need both of your help."* Daphne asks, *"how can we help?".* Dawn replies, *" I have a date with Prince Mason tonight."* Bethany asks stunned, *"Mason?".* Daphne is also surprised saying, *"I guess we both just figured it would be Ralph, not Mason you'd want to go on a date with".* Dawn says, *" I'd love to go on a date with Ralph too, but I need to explore the option of dating Mason".* Bethany asks, *"so, how do you need our help?".* Dawn says, *"I have no idea what to wear!".* Daphne excitedly says, *"YES!!! give me five minutes in your closet!".* Daphne runs into the closet and soon comes out. Dawn tries out three outfits and eventually chooses a pink lace romper; Bethany says, *"it's perfect for you."* Dawn smiles and thanks them while Daphne and Bethany does her hair and makeup. Daphne asks, *"are you ready to go for your date?".* Daphne replies, *"hmm.. I'm not sure. am I making a mistake?".* Daphne asks, *"do YOU think you are?".* Bethany says, *"you'll never know if you don't atleast try it."* Dawn says, *"you're both right".* There is a knock on the door and Dawn heads out. Bethany says, *"this isn't going to go well."* Daphne asks, *"why not?".* Bethany replies, *"I think we both know she's meant to be with Ralph. I'm not a Mason fan."* Daphne says, *"something tells me that Mason is because of grandmother, you do NOT disobey her ever".* Bethany says, *"well, I hope Dawn learns to stand up and say no".*

Chapter 19

At the restaurant, Dawn was surprised by the lighting, decorations and rose petals saying, *"Mason, this place is gorgeous".* Mason says, *"I picked it just for you, I wanted to make sure you had a great first date with me."* Dawn blushes saying, *"aww, I appreciate that".* Mason and Dawn sit and order their dinner, they chat and get to know each other better, Dawn thinks, *'who would have thought Mason was a kind gentleman? It was nice getting to know each other and I learned he was an only child too and also about his interest and family'.* After dinner, Dawn and Mason take a walk down the park; Dawn laughs hearing one of Mason's stories from college days. Mason says, *"thanks you Dawn for giving me a chance to take you out".* Dawn says, *"sure".* Mason asks, *"do you mind if I ask you a question?".* Dawn replies, *"of course, ask away".* Mason asks, *"what do you want from your future at the castle?".* Dawn replies, *"I, actually don't know, I haven't really thought about it."* Mason asks, *"well, then what are you original thoughts?".* Dawn replies, *"hmmm... I guess on the surface, I want to do right by the people, I just hope I don't take over for a long time."* Mason says, *"when you do take over, I know you will be a wonderful Queen".* Dawn says, *"I seriously cannot imagine being a Queen."* Mason teases her and she laughs calling him a *'weirdo'.* Dawn says, *"I want to see my parents happy".* Mason asks, *"what do you mean by that Dawn?".* Dawn replies, *"whatever their happiness is, whether together or with others, I want that for them".* Mason asks, *"you don't think, they are happy? why?".* Dawn answers, *"maybe they are, if they are great and if not then...".* Mason asks, *"is someone a bit of a hopeless romantic?".* Dawn giggles replies, *"perhaps I am".* Mason says, *"a good thing for me to remember for the future".* Mason asks, *"any other desires for the future".* Dawn answers, *" well... um... I guess I just want to build better relationship with everyone in my family. I mean, I'm close with my mom, but I am still learning more about my dad, cousins, and grandmother. I would love to get closer to everyone, including Charlie".* Mason brings her home and kisses her cheek, wishes her goodnight, and says, " *I hope you had fun and hope you'd consider a second date with me?".* Dawn says, *"um... I'm not sure Mason".* Mason asks, *"why not? didn't you enjoy our date?".* Dawn replies, " *I did, but I just... I don't know."* Mason says, *"I have an idea.. let me take you out on one more date, I can prove to you the kind of guy I am and how serious I am about you".* Dawn nervously nods saying, *"sure".* He leaves while Dawn heads back into her room however is stunned to find Ralph waiting for her. She says, *"Ralph, you scared me!".* Ralph apologises and bows greeting her. Dawn asks, *"can I help you, Ralph?".* Ralph replies, *"I just came with a message for from the Queen".* Dawn says, *"oh, what is it?".* Ralph says, *"she just wanted to remind you of your training starting an hour later tomorrow morning."* Dawn thanks Ralph while he sees her dressed up asking, *"where were you?".* Dawn replies, *"out".* Ralph says, *"out? with who? were you out with HIM??".*

Dawn ask, *"who is 'him'?".* Ralph angrily says, *"you know who 'him' is!".* Dawn says, *"not sure I do?".* Ralph says, *"Prince Mason".* Dawn says, *"Mason? yes, I was out with him".* Ralph asks, *"why?".* Dawn says, *"we went out on a date."* Ralph felt angry and said, *"you did WHAT???".* Dawn says, *"I... um...went...".* Ralph angrily says, *"are you kidding me??".* Dawn says, *"Ralph, why are you screaming at me?".* Ralph says, *"Dawn, I care about you! don't you see that?".* Dawn was stunned saying, *"oh, so that's what this is about?".* Ralph says, *"of course that's what this is about!".* Dawn says angrily, *"RALPH! don't you get it?".* Ralph asks, *"what?".* Dawn says, " *we couldn't be together even if we wanted to! our positions won't ever allow it- whether we both want it or not!".* Ralph's expression changes to sadness while Dawn realises the harshness of her words. Dawn says, *"Ralph... I'm sorry.. that's not what I meant".* Ralph says, *"no... you're right, Princess, I don't know what I was thinking and why I was hopeful, but I apologise for crossing my boundaries".* He leaves the room as Dawn tries calling him back however breaks down crying before falling asleep. A few months pass, Dawn has been studying hard and also taking extra lessons from Mason. Mason asks, *"so Dawn, any reply yet to our second date?"*. Dawn replies, *"I... um... can't sorry Mason"*. Mason tries to push for an answer however Dawn says, *"I can't, please respect my decision"*. She leaves and heads to the living room where Bethany and Daphne are watching a movie. Dawn sits with them and hangs out; Daphne says, *"we need to plan a party"*. Dawn says, *"Daph, I'm not really a party person"*. Daphne says, *"Dawn, you need to learn to especially as it's part of being a royal"*. Meanwhile, Charlie watched the girls and left; soon that afternoon, Dawn came to the garden and thought, *'why am I still in pain? my heart hurts so much.. I hurt Ralph... his eyes are full of pain and sadness because of me... I wish I wasn't a Princess'*. Amelia comes over to Dawn saying, *"Dawn? are you ok?"*.

Dawn replies, *"I'm good mom."* Amelia senses Dawn's sadness however Dawn insists she's ok and walks away. Dawn comes to the pond, feeds the ducks and sighs. Daniel comes over and says, *"hi, Dawn"*. Dawn says, *"oh, hey dad"*. Daniel asks, *"are you ok?"*. Dawn replies, *"I'm not sure"*. She takes a deep breath while Daniel asks, *"do you want to talk about it?"*. Daniel says, *" if you need help, talk to me or your mom, we only want your happiness"*. Dawn nods saying, *"dad, I'm so confused and overwhelmed. I may have feelings for Ralph, but I know we would have a huge battle ahead of us and grandmother wants me to see if I could possibly have feelings for Prince Mason too. although she doesn't know about Ralph because I'm too afraid to tell her about it. but I hurt Ralph saying cruel words and I don't think he will forgive me even if I ask him to. I just feel conflicted between the two and this situation."* Daniel says, *"Dawn, every good thing in life will come with struggle and heartache, it's how you face these battles that defines the outcome; if you're confused, why don't you take a trip, sort it out in your head"*. Dawn says, *"that would be a great idea, dad!"*. Daniel says, *" but I have a request?"*. Dawn asks, *"which is?"*. Daniel replies, *"Ralph, Mason, Charlie, Bethany and Daphne will go with you too; it'll be a little holiday for you all and it'll give you the chance to spend time with the guys and get to know them better away from the castle however, nothing should happen!".* Dawn asks, *"what do you mean by that dad?".* Daniel replies, *"no kissing and definitely maintain your innocence. oh no, have you lost it?".* Dawn gives her dad a cold stare replying, *"first of all, no I have not. and even I did, I would never tell you. but the answer is no, and I am still 'innocent'."* Daniel says, *"hmmm, ok".* Dawn laughs and says, *"so about the trip?".*

Daniel says, *"I have to persuade your mom and grandmother".* Dawn says, *"even if you can't, I really appreciate the thought, just getting away and having some time to think might be what I need";* Dawn hugs her dad and heads back to her room to rest.

Chapter 20

Daniel comes to meet Amelia who is in the garden reading a book. Daniel says, *"Amy, come with me. we need to talk"*. Soon on the terrace, Amelia looks around asking, *"so Danny, why did you bring me here?"*. Daniel replies, *"well, our daughter told me that she is having a bit of a disaster"*. Amelia looks sadly, *"oh"*. Daniel says, *"she is confused and needs a break"*. Amelia asks, *"confused about what?"*. Daniel replies, *"boys?"*. Amelia says sadly, *"she opened up to you about this?"*. Daniel says, *"yes, but I pushed her to talk. you have to know, she loves you."* Amelia asks, *"why won't she talk to me anymore? we used to tell each other everything. now she barely speaks to me"*. Daniel hugs Amelia saying, *"Amelia, I promise you are not losing her, she is just overwhelmed."* Amelia says, *"I know, I just hope she's ok"*. Daniel says, *"she is, I'm here now to help both of you and I won't be leaving either of you anytime soon"*. Daniel kisses Amelia warmly as she hugs him. Amelia asks, *"what were you saying about Dawn?"*. Daniel replies, *"I think it might be best if we send her and some of the other kids away for the weekend."* Amelia asks stunned, *"away?"*. Daniel replies, *"I just think she needs space from this environment to think about her feelings and more"*. Amelia says, *"I am worried about sending her away"*. Daniel says, *"I plan to send Ralph, Charlie, Mason, Daphne, and Bethany with her. if that helps and of course the guards, I wouldn't let those kids go anywhere without a guard. they will be a safe distance and the kids will be fine"*. Amelia nods saying, *"ok, I agree that they can go"*. Daniel smiles saying, *"now I just have to get mom's approval"*. Amelia rolls her eyes saying, *"she will never agree with this"*. Daniel says, *"I have a trick up my sleeve"*. Daniel kisses Amelia's cheek and heads back inside. Daniel comes to the study and says, *"mom, I need to talk to you"*. Queen Matilda says, *"of course Daniel, what is it?"*. Daniel says, *"sorry to bother you mom, Dawn has been working really hard lately".* Queen Matilda nods saying, *"she has, I have been very impressed with her".* Daniel smiles and says, *" I was thinking, she deserves a little break this weekend, does she not?".* Queen Matilda asks, *"a break?".* Daniel says, *"mom she's been here since her mom went to the hospital, she's been working hard, and I can tell she is worn out".*

Queen Matilda asks, *"and you think a weekend vacation will do the trick?".* Daniel says, *" mom, she has been non-stop learning about being a Princess ever since she found out. I think she deserves a little break even if it is just a weekend."* Queen Matilda thinks for a moment while Daniel says, *"she won't be alone if you are worried, she will be with Ralph, Daphne, Bethany, Charlie, and Mason. Dawn seems to have taken a liking to Prince Mason.it may be a good way for them to bond a little more."* Queen Matilda says, *"that would be a perfect idea, Daniel; go ahead and tell everyone to pack up and we can send them to our private island, it's protected there".* Daniel says, *" that's exactly what I was thinking. a weekend at the beach resort will be perfect."* Queen Matilda gives her approval and leaves. Soon, Daniel knocks on Dawn's door; she wakes up and opens to see her dad. He comes in and gives her the good news. Dawn says surprised and excited, *"omg, mom and grandma agreed?".* Daniel nods, *"yeah, they did".* Dawn hugs her dad happily and jumps excitedly. Dawn stops for a moment and looks her dad nervously who laughs saying, *"you need a break, you need to clear your head".* Dawn asks, *"where are we going?".* Daniel says, *"that's a surprise but you'll love it. you will leave tonight".* Daniel turns to go while Dawn says, *"dad I don't know what to pack!".* He says, *"think tropical summer and beach and also call Beth, she's going too".* Dawn looks at the time and starts packing. Soon in the private jet, Bethany asks, *"I wonder, where we are heading to?".* Dawn replies, *"I'm not sure Beth, dad didn't tell me".* Daphne says, *"I am super excited about this trip!".* Dawn asks, *"Daph, do you have a clue where we are going?".* Daphne shakes her head, *"nope, Uncle Daniel didn't tell me either".* Charlie rolls his eyes while Dawn is unbothered when he claims to know where they are heading off to. Ralph says, *"we will be heading to the Island".* Dawn was surprised and excited, *"Island?".* Bethany was stunned asking, *"what Island?".* Ralph asks, *"did you not know the royal family has their own island?".* Dawn says, *"we do?".* Daphne says, *"oh yeah! I forgot we do!".* Bethany is excited and yells, *"party on the island!".* Dawn says, *"I can't wait for some beach time!!!".* Soon they reach the resort as Dawn takes a second to admire the view. Mason watches her thinking, *'this could be the perfect place to see how she feels about me.'* Mason says, *"hey Dawn, what do you think of the island?".* Dawn replies, *"it's incredible".* Mason asks, *"everyone is thinking of heading to the beach, wanna come?".* Dawn nods, *"sure, I love the beach!".* He leaves while she heads in and changes into her swimsuit; at the beach, Bethany and Daphne wonder about Dawn who soon comes. They take selfies and chat just while Ralph comes over; Dawn blushes seeing Ralph in a casual outfit. Bethany says, *"it's totally obvious that you are crushing and interested in him".* Dawn tries to hide it, but Daphne says, *"omg, you are! it's so cute".* Dawn says, *"I am interested in Ralph but I also kind of like Mason too".* Bethany and Daphne roll their eyes saying, *"ugh".* Daphne asks, *"Beth, wanna go for a walk with me?".* Bethany nods and they head off; Ralph comes over and says, *"hey Dawn".* She says, *"hey to you too".* Ralph asks, *"are you having fun?".* Dawn replies, *"I love the beach! the sand and sea is so relaxing".* They both look at the sea as Ralph says, *"you do know that someday this entire island and beach will belong to you?".* Dawn giggles asking, *"are you quoting 'lion king' on me?".* Ralph laughs replying, *"not exactly, but it's true, this will all belong to you Princess".* Dawn says, *"I know Ralph".* Ralph asks, *"do you want this?".* Dawn looks at him sadly as he tries to change the subject however Dawn takes a deep breath saying, *"I just have so much to take in, I love what I am doing now but it can be overwhelming at time."* Ralph asks, *"can I tell you something that may sound harsh?".* Dawn nods as he takes a deep breath saying, *"I think you always use the excuse of feeling overwhelmed, but you need to turn around and take on the numerous*

challenges? you are a remarkable young woman Dawn and I know and believe you can do it!".

Dawn blushes and says, *"wow, Ralph"*. Ralph asks, *"are you sure I didn't sound rude or harsh?".* Dawn replies, *"no, I think it's amazing that you are supportive of me".* Ralph smiles and says, *"just call me your cheerleader or fan, I care very deeply for you. how much of a guard for you would I be if I didn't give you a pep talk every now and again?".* Dawn smiles while Ralph asks, *" can I ask you something else Dawn? please be honest".* Ralph asks, *"do you care or have feelings for me?".* Dawn looked at Ralph thinking, *'oh boy'.*

Chapter 21

Dawn says, *"I do like you, Ralph very much, but I do have feelings for Mason too and I need to explore that."* Ralph nods and smiles at Dawn who says, *"I am glad you are so understanding"*. Ralph says, *"this place is so beautiful, and I would really like to ask you out on a date"*. Dawn says, *"really? I would like that very much"*. Ralph says, *"oh my, that's perfect.. I mean.. I would like to take you out on a date on this trip"*. Ralph removes his shirt while Dawn blushes and he says, *"the water is calling for me"*. He runs and jumps in. Mason comes behind Dawn as she turns and says, *"you scared me Mason!"*. He apologises and asks, *"are you having a nice time?"*. Dawn replies, *"of course, this place is amazing!"*. Mason says, *"Dawn, I would really like to take you out on our second date"*. Dawn says, *"I would very much love that"*. Mason asks, *"can you answer a question for me?"*. Dawn nods while he takes a breath asking, *"why have you been avoiding this second date with me?"*. Dawn replies, *"honestly, I have been feeling so overwhelmed and stressed lately, but I assure you I won't let that influence me anymore."* Mason says, *"I have to go but I look forward to our date tomorrow night"*. Dawn blushes and she watches Mason run off. It soon begins to get dark; Dawn thinks, *'I should get some sleep, it's been a long day of travelling and sun, maybe I could read my favourite book, 'Monsters of the Night'.* She comes back to the resort, into her room and says shocked, *"WHAT THE HELL???"*. Daphne and Bethany both stop kissing and look at her. Dawn asks, *"would one of you care to explain what the hell is going on?"*. Daphne says nervously, *"um...er... oh..."*. Bethany says, *"we're dating"*. Daphne says, *"way to be subtle!"*. Dawn asks surprised, *"um...what?"*. Daphne says, *"we're dating!"*. Dawn says still in shock, *"what? when? why? how? please explain this to me!"*.

Bethany says, *"fine but you need to calm down first".* Dawn takes a deep breath and hears Bethany and Daphne talk about their growing relationship. Dawn asks, *"how long has this been going on?".* Daphne replies, *"um... two months, do you approve of us?".* Dawn replies, *"it's not that, I am just surprised and shock".* Bethany says, *"we've had to hide it!".* Daphne sighs saying, *" no one in our family will understand".* Dawn asks, *"why not?".* Daphne explains how orthodox the family is and Dawn understands. She asks, *"are you both gay?".* Bethany replies, *"I'm bisexual".* Daphne replies, *"I am not sure, still kind of deciding and figuring things out".* Dawn nods while Bethany asks, *"are you ok with this?".* Dawn answers, *"if you're happy, I am happy. I just wasn't expecting this at all".* Daphne asks, *"can you please not tell anyone right now?".* Dawn says stunned, *" do you really think I would tell your secret. it's not my place to tell anything".* Daphne says, *"thanks, we will tell everyone in our own time".* Dawn says, *"I understand, can we change the topic? I have a date?".* Bethany asks, *"with Ralph, right?".* Dawn nods as Bethany cheers. Dawn says, *"I also have a date with Mason".* Daphne says, *"I knew she'd go for the route of her country".* Bethany and Daphne have a small argument however Dawn says, *"I am going on a date with Mason tomorrow night and then Ralph the following night".* Bethany and Daphne both have questions for Dawn about the two guys. She thinks, *'they are both different and each have a special quality like Mason is funny and we enjoy each other's company. Ralph is supportive, kind and gentlemen".* Dawn says, *"Ralph is like my version of music.. sweet classical".* Daphne asks confused, *"what do you mean by classical music?".* Bethany explains and Daphne finds it sweet, Dawn yawns, Bethany asks, *"Daph, let's head to the beach for a walk".* Daphne replies, *"sure thing bee".* Dawn says, *"bee?".* Bethany says, *"her nickname for me. I like it!".* Bethany wishes Dawn goodnight and heads out; Daphne thanks Dawn for her support, hugs her and wishes her goodnight. The next day, Ralph meets Bethany and asks, *"I need your help with planning my date for Dawn".* Bethany agrees as they head back inside to discuss things privately. Later that evening, Dawn dresses in a black lace dress; she sees Mason waiting for her and they head off for dinner. Dawn says, *"Mason, dinner has been most delightful. this must all be expensive"*. Mason says, *"aww Princess, don't worry about cost... you're priceless"*. Dawn giggles just as Mason gets up asking, *"would you like to take a walk in the garden?"*. Dawn smiles, nods and they head off. Mason says, *"tonight has been amazing, I am really happy you agreed to this second date with me. can I kiss you, Dawn?"*.

Dawn was stunned by Mason's request and replies, *"I would like a kiss, but do you mind if we wait for a bit?"*. Mason asks, *"what's up?"*. Dawn says, *"I just want to be more committed to you before I kiss you"*. Mason asks, *"are we not committed?"*. Dawn shakes her head while Mason takes a deep breath saying, *"I promise if you let me in as your boyfriend, I will always treat you like the Princess you truly are. you are beautiful and I would feel sad if I didn't atleast tell you I want that chance to be yours"*. Dawn says, *" I appreciate that, but I really want the opportunity to think, I just got the chance to be a Princess, I'm still learning and trying to be the best version of myself. if you can give me time to think about your offer, I would love that."* Mason agrees to give her time and they soon head back. The next evening, Dawn had her date with Ralph who organised a picnic on the beach. Dawn says, *"this is so perfect"*. They sit, eat and chat; Ralph says, *"I am so happy you gave me a chance Dawn"*. Dawn smiles and takes Ralph's hand. She says, *"it wouldn't be fair if I ignored your request"*. Ralph says, *"I adore you Dawn, you're like Aphrodite"*. Dawn gets up and walks towards the water, she extends her hand to Ralph who takes it and pulls her closer; they have a moment. Ralph says, *"Dawn, if you choose me, I promise to always be there for you, I want to be by your side supporting you as a cheerleader. I want you to believe in yourself and be the unstoppable force, I hope you will give me that chance"*. Dawn giggles and blushes hearing Ralph's word saying, *"you're incredibly sweet, Ralph, you are such a kind soul"*. He says, *"I love you more than you can ever imagine Dawn, I hope you believe me *when I say that, if you don't choose me it's ok, all I want is your happiness".* Dawn says, *"I really like you Ralph, can you give me the time to think about it until we get back?".* Ralph nods replying, *"sure, Dawn".* Ralph looks at the sky, Dawn turns and sees a shower of shooting stars; they both close their eyes and make a wish.

Chapter 22

Ralph and Dawn head back to the resort; Dawn blushes and says, *"thank you so much, Ralph, I had a great time tonight"*. Mason says, *"excuse me Dawn?! what?"*. He angrily looks at her while Ralph says, *"jealous, Prince?"*. Dawn says, *"listen guys, I am not about to have fight on my hands here, I am not officially dating either of you. I need to think now. so yeah, goodnight"*. Dawn leaves while Mason says angrily, *"who the hell do you think you are? what do you think you are doing?"*. Ralph replies, *"trying to be the best man I can be."* Mason warns Ralph, *"you stay away from her, she's going to be my girlfriend."* Ralph says, *"oh, as far as I'm aware, she hasn't decided that yet"*. Mason says furiously, *"YOU ARE THE HELP! YOU ARE NOT OF HER STATUS AND NOT WORTHY OF HER! get it through your dumb head and leave her alone"*. Ralph says, *"no, I will not. I will fight for her"*. Mason says, *"you'll regret this"*. Mason leaves and heads to Charlie's room. he says, *"bro, we have a problem"*. Charlie says, *"what's up?"*.

Mason replies, *"that man servant Ralph is trying to get Dawn's attention too."* Charlie rolls his unbothered while Mason says, *"I want Dawn and I refuse to let him win"*. Charlie says, *"prove to her that you deserve her"*. Charlie thinks of something before heading to sleep. Mason says, *"really, I have to wait until morning for your plan"*. The next day, Dawn is her room in deep thoughts, *'I really need to decide, maybe it was a bad idea to have the guys here while I thought things through however the dates really made this trip special'*. She calls her dad and asks, *"dad, can I stay here for a few extra hours?"*. Daniel replies concerned, *"is everything ok, Princess?"*. Dawn replies, *"yeah, I just need some space"*. Daniel allows and says, *" ok, I will let the pilot send the jet to you later after bringing everyone back first"*. Dawn says, *"thanks dad, love you"*. Dawn tells everyone to get ready as they head to the airport however

Dawn goes to the beach and thinks, *'I need to think about this, Mason or Ralph'.* Soon back in the castle, Charlie asks, *"Mason, are you sure you are ready for this?".* Mason replies, *"why won't I be?".* Charlie says, *"time to regain your woman".* Charlie knocks on the door and enters with Mason to see Queen Matilda who is surprised to see them. Queen Matilda asks, *"to what do I owe this pleasure?".* Mason says, *"well, Your Majesty as you know Dawn and I have been kind of seeing each other for a while without telling the family."* Queen Matilda smiles saying, *"I am pleased to hear that, I was confident you would be a good match for my granddaughter".* Mason says, *"problem is, she is starting to develop feelings for someone else".* Queen Matilda's smile drops, and she gives a stern look at the guys. Mason says, *"I am not happy about it either".* Queen Matilda, asks, *"who is he?".* Mason replies, *"Ralph, the right-hand man to King Daniel".* Queen Matilda says, *"what!".* Charlie says, *"it's true, I've seen them myself".* Queen Matilda says, *"this is absolutely ridiculous and unacceptable!".*

Mason is glad that Queen Matilda agrees with him. She says, *"I refuse to let my grandchild be with someone of lower status".* Charlie says, *"grandma, if I may say a word?".* Queen Matilda nods while Charlie says, *"fire him, you have the authority and right. she won't see him if you remove him from the castle and banish him from the kingdom and in his absence, Mason will be there to provide the comfort and friendship she needs".* Queen Matilda says, *"that is a great idea, Charlie".* He thanks her; Mason says, *"I need to be ready to see her when she lands, and it should be done before she returns".* Queen Matilda says, *" let me handle that part, I will fire him shortly, take you leave now and send him to me".* Charlie and Mason both bow replying, *"as you wish and thank you once again Your Majesty".* Elsewhere, Dawn was still thinking, *'both the guys are great, I like Mason... he makes me laugh and I enjoy his company.. but do I like him because I want to do right by my country? however he has a dark side and dark history too... then there's Ralph.. he's a sweetheart.. someone who has always been by my side.. he makes my dark days feel so bright... Ralph is the music to my heart... that's it... it's Ralph! it's always meant to be Ralph!. I need to head home and talk to Mason and Ralph'.* Dawn heads back and rushes to the airport. Meanwhile, Ralph comes to see Queen Matilda and bow asking, *"Your Highness, you called?".* The Queen says, *"yes, Raphael. I need to ask you to leave".* Ralph was stunned as Queen Matilda said, *"we have decided we no longer need your services, and you must leave".* Ralph asks, *"may I please ask what I have done?".* Queen Matilda says, *"as much as I would love to give you some kind of explanation, no. you must go. now!. you have two hours to pack and remove yourself, you are not welcome on the grounds of the castle, nor are you welcome anywhere in the kingdom".* Ralph says, *"what! wait, so not only are you firing me, but you are also banishing me too?".* Queen Matilda says, *"of course, you can't believe I would let you stay here if you're being relieved of your duty?".* Ralph looks sadly saying, *"please Your Highness, reconsider your decision".* Ralph thinks, *'how will I tell Dawn?".* Queen Matilda replies, *"no, I have made my decision. now leave... you only have two hours, and you are wasting it".* Ralph bows before leaving while Queen Matilda says, *"good riddance!".* Ralph heads to his room and begins to pack thinking, *'I'd better pack... I have to tell Dawn about this... without getting caught.. I'll send a letter through Beth..'.* Ralph finishes packing and writing the letter; He finds Bethany in the living room and says, *"Beth, I need your help!".* Bethany asks, *"Ralph, are you ok?".* Ralph replies, *"look, I don't have time to explain, but I am leaving, and I need you to do me a huge favour, please".* Bethany was stunned by Ralph's word as he hands her an envelope and says, *"please, make sure Dawn gets this note".* Bethany nods and says, *"I will Ralph, but please don't leave".* Ralph sadly says, *"I don't have a choice".* Bethany hugs Ralph wishing him luck while Ralph says, *"take care of Dawn".* Bethany promises and soon watches Ralph leave; a few hours later, Dawn comes home and greets her parents. She hugs them both happily and then asks, *"do you know where Mason and Ralph are?".* Daniel replies, *"sorry sweetie, I haven't seen them in a while actually".* Queen Matilda comes there and says, *"hi everyone, I have some bad news to tell you."* Dawn asks, *"what is it?"*.

Queen Matilda says, *"I found out some very sad news about Ralph today, it turns out he was stealing from the castle- so I fired him."* Dawn was shocked asking, *"how could he do something like that?"*. Daniel asks, *"mom, are you sure?"*. Queen Matilda replies, *"sadly, I am"*. Daniel didn't buy into it; Dawn asks, *"grandma, where is he?"*. Queen Matilda replies, *"he was given two hours to pack and leave, he's been gone for several hours now"*. Amelia says, *"Dawn, I am sorry, Princess"*. Dawn felt anger in her eyes saying, *"I can't believe him! I almost chose him, and he lied to me!"*. Dawn runs off crying while Amelia tries to call out to her. Amelia cries while Daniel hugs her. Amelia says, *"she never wishes to talk to me Daniel"*. Daniel says, *"give her a moment, she's just had a huge shock, she loved him Amelia."* Amelia says, *"I know"*. Soon in her room, Queen Matilda comes to check on Dawn who has been crying unconsolably. Queen Matilda says, *"Dawn, I only did what was right."* Dawn says, *"it doesn't matter, ok! you win"*. Queen Matilda asks confused, *"win? what are you talking about?"*.

Chapter 23

D awn says, *"don't you know that I tried to like Mason for you??"*. Queen Matilda asks, *"why wouldn't you like him?, he's handsome, kind, well-spoken and he's a Prince"*. Dawn rolls her eyes just as Queen Matilda says, *"do not roll your eyes at me, young lady"*. Dawn says, *"I tried, ok! but I fell in love with Ralph along the way! and now? he's a crook and I am devasted, angry and can't believe I fell for this stupid charade! how could I be so stupid?"*. She cries while Queen Matilda says, *"Dawn... sometimes life has a funny way of teaching us lessons we never thought we needed. maybe this one was that you shouldn't trust love.."*. Dawn asks, *"how can you not trust love?"*. Queen Matilda says, *"look sweetheart, I didn't marry for love. I married for what was right for my country. but without that- I wouldn't have had the life I had, and you know what, I did grow to love my husband. I know it's hard to hear this now, but please give Mason a chance to prove he is worthy of your love"*. Queen Matilda suggests to clear the air; Dawn nods and says, *"ok"*. She heads into the shower, changes, and thinks, *'I don't have much of a choice now....'* She heads into the garden and sees Mason sitting by the flowers. Mason says, *"hey Dawn"*. Dawn says, *"hey"*. Mason asks, *"are you ok?"*. Dawn says, *"you know what? I'm great.. I'm sure you heard about Ralph, and I'm sad about that but I am fine"*. Mason smiles at her and then asks, *"did you happen to make a decision?"*. Dawn nods and says, *"I choose you"*. Mason was surprised asking, *"you did?"*. She blushes and says, *"I did"*. Mason was excited and comes closer taking her in his arms. He says, *"can I kiss my girlfriend now?"*. Dawn was hesitant replying, *"I have never been kissed before"*. He comes closer and kisses her warmly. Dawn blushes while Mason says, *"I promise to always kiss you like this, Dawn. I promise to make you happy for as long as you'll have me, and I promise that I will treat you like the Queen you will be one day"*. Dawn smiles happily while Mason checks the time and says, *"I have a few things to do but I think we should do something to celebrate tonight"*. Dawn says, *"I look forward to it, Mase"*. Mason kisses her again before leaving. Dawn's smile drops for a moment wondering, *'why do I feel so upset about this first kiss? why do I feel it shouldn't have been him? it's time to move on from Ralph and focus on Mason... but why does my heart not accept it?'*. Bethany comes to see Dawn asking, *"bestie, are you ok?"*. Dawn replies, *"yeah, I'm fine"*. Bethany asks, *"what's going on?"*. Dawn says, *"I'm dating Mason now"*. Bethany asks, *"I thought you would choose Ralph"*. Dawn says, *"I wanted too but he was caught stealing and my grandmother fired him"*. Bethany was shocked while Dawn says, *"I feel so upset and sad. how could he do this?"*. Bethany thought for a minute and said, *"Dawn, I feel like something fishy is going on"*. Dawn doesn't agree while Bethany has her doubts saying, *"I don't believe Ralph could do something like that. he wouldn't steal or put his job at risk."* Dawn says, *"maybe"*. She sighs while Bethany says, *"this is from Ralph"*. She takes the envelope asking, *"what is this, Beth?"*. Bethany replies, *"a letter"*. Dawn says, *"I may need to read this alone, Beth"*. Bethany nods and leaves her to her thoughts. Dawn cries thinking, *'why did he do this to me? why did he have to steal and leave? I love him so much... I think I always will.... Ralph...I guess life will change for me now...'* Dawn still holds the letter and says, *"I don't think I can read this letter... not yet..."* She puts it in her pocket and looks at the sky wondering, *'I wonder what will happen now...I guess only time will tell....'* Five years pass; Dawn is looking out from her balcony and tells, *'so much has changed in these five years... Daphne and Bethany are still dating happily... they haven't told anybody and kept it secret... Charlie hasn't change except he parties more... something happened a year ago... my grandmother... Queen Matilda passed it was a sudden illness which took her away from us... my dad was affected the worst.. mom and dad got married and took over the kingdom... Mason comes every now and again... he's got a duty to his country however he tells me that my country and family feels more like home to him...'.* Dawn has a smile on her face when Mason comes behind her saying, *"hello, my beautiful fiancée".* Dawn turns and blushes thinking, *' oh, Mason and I are engaged to be married soon. In six months', time, he, and I will be crowned Prince and Princess... I couldn't be more excited'.* Dawn kisses Mason saying, *"my handsome hunky fiancée".* Mason says, *"I can't wait to marry you, Princess."* Dawn says, *"mmmm mmmm.... me too my Prince".* Later that afternoon, Dawn was discussing wedding plan ideas with Bethany. Dawn says, *"ok, you and Daphne will be by my side. Mason told me he has Charlie as his best man".* Daphne soon comes and joins them while Dawn continues explaining details. Daphne asks, *"are you sure about this?".* Bethany replies, *"I've asked that many times too, Daph".* Dawn says, *"of course I am, I love him, and we've been together for five years. it's about time to take this next step in our relationship".* Bethany says, *"I don't like how you say it".* Dawn says, *"say what?".* Daphne and Bethany answer together, *"it's time to take the next step in our relationship, it makes us think you're doing this because of timing. you are still young, and you can find someone else".* Dawn rolls her eyes saying, *"I don't want to, I've told you both so many times... I love Mason".* Before an argument can happen; Dawn takes a deep breath and gets back to planning wedding ideas. Daphne asks, *"have you chosen your theme yet?".* Dawn replies, *"I have but I'm not sure if it will be ok".* Bethany asks, *"why not?".* Dawn says, *"I really like the idea of something simple yet elegant".* Daphne adores the idea however Dawn says, *"I don't think the kingdom will, we are joining two kingdoms in this union".* Bethany says, *"so what? it's your special day. you should choose whatever makes you happy".* Dawn says, *"Mason is the opposite... he wants something big and since I've got my choice to marry here, I thought I should be fair and give him his wish".* Meanwhile back inside, Amelia and Daniel were in the living room waiting for someone. Amelia asks, *"are we sure about bringing him back here, Danny?".* Daniel replies, *"Amy, something tells me this is not what we originally thought it to be".* Amelia asks, *"but what about Dawn?".* Daniel replies, *"we will cross that bridge when we get there".* Amelia says, *"let's agree that I think this could be a bad mistake for Dawn's sake".* Daniel nods just as the door opens and a familiar face enters the room.

Chapter 24

Ralph enters and bows saying, *"Your Highnesses".* Daniel says, *"Ralph, good to have you back here".* Ralph says, *"it was nice to receive your letter asking for my attendance today".* Daniel says, *"we just wanted to discuss a few things with you".* Ralph says, *"ok".* Elsewhere, Dawn was feeding the ducks in the pond and thinking about her wedding, *'I really need to get everything ready... what colours sound good? emerald...pearl...'.* However, her thoughts were interrupted when she heard a familiar voice behind her. Ralph says, *"Princess Dawn".* Dawn got up, turned for a moment and was about to fall into the pond however Ralph held her hand and pulled her close. Dawn was shocked to see Ralph and says stunned, *"R-Ralph?".* He bows and greets her, *"hello, Princess Dawn".* Dawn asks, *"w-what??w-what are you doing here?".* Ralph replies, *"your parents invited me to talk to them, it would have been disrespectful to ignore the request of the King and Queen".* Dawn nods while Ralph tries to says, *"um, Dawn-".* Dawn's face changes to anger replying, *"no, you don't get to call me that!".* Ralph sadly says, *"oh- I just thought-".* Dawn says, *"well, you thought wrong! Ralph- why are you back? what is your reason for returning?".* Ralph replies, *"your parents asked me to return to speak about what happened all those years ago".* Dawn says, *"I wish they could have spoken to me first".* Ralph says, *"with all due-respect, it's their call not yours".* Dawn rolls her eyes saying, *"I don't have to listen to this".* Ralph says, *"you don't but I didn't seek you out today. I don't really know why I'm here fully myself, but I came to speak to them. they asked me for some time, so I decided to take a walk out to here.. this used to be my favourite place in the castle, and I wanted to see if it still helped me calm down."* Dawn felt embarrassed while Ralph says, *"look, you don't have to like me, but I want to congratulate you on your engagement to Prince Mason, I wish you nothing but luck and love in*

78

your marriage". He soon leaves while Dawn thinks, *'oh my god! I cannot believe he is here right now... I thought I would never see him again...'.* Mason comes over saying, *"what the hell?".* Dawn was surprised to see Mason who says, *"what the hell is he doing back?".* Dawn replies, *"I am not sure, but my parents requested for him apparently".* Mason says, *"I don't like it".* Dawn agrees and says, *"look I will be talking to my parents about this later".* Mason feels a sense of relieve while Dawn teases him asking, *"you jealous, Mase?".* Mason says, *"don't try it Dawn. I hate that guy! he stole from your family? have you forgotten?".* Dawn says, *"I do! of course I do!".* Mason warns her, *"you are not speaking to him without me present. do I make myself clear?".* Dawn says annoyed, *" and why not?".* Mason answers, *"because I'm your fiancée and you should respect my wishes".* Dawn says, *" fine, I promise I will not speak with him unless I am with you, happy?".* Mason calms down and thanks her while Dawn leaves to go speak with her parents. Dawn comes inside thinking, *'I can't believe they would do this! after all this time, how can they trust him?'.* Just then Dawn sees a door opened and hears her dad saying, *"Ralph, I am grateful you came today".* Dawn thinks, *'I can hear them! I could eavesdrop but that wouldn't be very Princessy. who am I kidding? I'm going to listen in'.* Daniel says, *"Ralph, we never really had the opportunity to ask you exactly what happened that day."* Ralph says, *"honestly, I don't exactly know".* Amelia says, *"we were informed that you stole from the crown".* Ralph was shocked and says, *"what? excuse me? I would never do that, I respected you sire far more than a boss. I saw you as a friend and father-figure. I would never do anything do ruin that".* Daniel says, *"I believe and trust you, Ralph".* Amelia agrees too leaving Ralph surprised. Daniel asks, *"do you know why it would be said that you were stealing?".* Ralph answers, *"to be honest, no."* Daniel wonders and says, *"I am curious if this has anything to do with Dawn?".* Amelia agrees while Ralph asks, *"in what way, sire?".* Amelia says, *"you got very close to Dawn right before you were fired, weren't you?".* Ralph nods while Daniel says, *"I think the Queen may have found out and decided to end it her own way".* Outside Dawn thinks angrily, *'oh, hell, no grandma! you did not mess and interfere with my love life! I have to talk to Daphne and Bethany about this!'.* Daniel says, "I think for now, it might be best if we kept this between us three." Ralph asks nervously, "um what about Dawn?". Daniel says, "let's not tell her yet, I think we need to figure out what happened before we say anything to her. This could be a serious problem if this gets out." Ralph nods sadly while outside Dawn thinks, *'not acceptable. I must speak with Daphne and Bethany! now!'.* She leaves while back inside Ralph asks, "if I may be so bold as to speak openly? I think Mason had something to do with it'. Daniel and Amelia were stunned while Daniel says, "that is our future son-in-law, so tread softly here". Ralph says, "I mean no disrespect, I just find it strange that he found out about us and then I was fired". Daniel says, "that is strange...'. Ralph says, " if I can continue with something that may not go well?". Daniel nods just as Ralph says, "well....I am still in love with Dawn". Amelia asks, "you are?". Ralph says, "yes, I know she's in love with someone else, but I've never stopped loving her, I just want to know if I have your blessing to let her know how I feel?". Amelia excitedly says, "yes! Please do!". Daniel says, "hold on Amy! Ralph, I will give you my blessing, but I want to warn you. Dawn truly loves Mason; you can't have any expectations of her. is that clear to you?". Ralph nods and understands saying, "I just need to know how she feels about me before I can move forward with my life whether that is here or not". Daniel says, "I can tell you that you are not going to be welcomed here by Mason or the others. In fact, knowing Mason he will not allow you to speak with Dawn at all however I have a plan for how to allow you access to Dawn",. Ralph smiles and says, "ok sire, let's talk". Elsewhere, Dawn was in her room thinking, *'I cannot believe this! who would do this to him? what if it's all a lie? a way to get back at the kingdom....'.* There is a knock on the door, Bethany and Daphne come in. Bethany says, "hey bestie". Daphne says, "you asked to see us? is everything ok?". Dawn says, "Ralph is back". They were both surprised and happy however Bethany noticed that Dawn was sad and asked, *"why are you so unhappy about it?".* Dawn sighs replying, *"I'm not upset about his return. it's what recently I overheard about his dismissal which makes me angry. it turns out that grandma lied to us about why Ralph was fired in the first place, it turns out he didn't steal at all".* Daphne says stunned, *"What?".* Bethany says, *"I knew it".* Daphne says, *"poor Ralph, did he know about the theft accusation?".* Dawn replies, *"no he didn't".* Bethany says, *"I tried to explain and tell you about this Dawn".*

Chapter 25

Daphne soon gets a call and leaves. Bethany asks, *"Dawn, have you read his letter yet?".* Dawn replies, *"I have no intention of reading it."* Bethany says, *"it's been five years, you have to".* Dawn rolls her eyes and says, *"no I'm not reading it and I don't have to do anything".* Beth says, *"you really need to know what he said".* Dawn snaps at Bethany who says, *"Dawn, he loved you then and I doubt he stopped, you should read it and just be prepared. You know he'll ask you if you have read it, he'll ask me if I gave it to you and I won't lie to him".* Dawn says, *"fine, I'll read it".* Bethany understands Dawn needs to do this alone and says, *"I look forward to hearing what it say later."* Bethany left while Dawn thought, *'am I really going to do this?'.* Dawn opened a drawer and took out the envelope in her hands. She felt afraid, nervous but also excited as she slowly opened the envelope and began to read the letter:

My Dearest Princess Dawn,

I am so incredibly sorry; I am sorry I wasn't home when you returned. I am not sure what happened, and I don't have a lot of time to explain- but I have been relieved of my duties. I will no longer be at the castle and sadly I am not allowed to come back either. I pray someday I can return to you, and I hope you don't forget me in the meantime. but know this, I love you. I always have and I honestly believe I always will. I can actually promise you that I always will. Please be strong, become the leader I know you can be. always know that I am your biggest cheerleader and fan, be independent, believe in yourself, be powerful but most importantly, be you.

Sincerely, Ralph

Dawn began to cry feeling a wave of emotions. She thought, *'why am I crying so much? is the fact I didn't trust Ralph and believed my grandma over him? I am so sorry Ralph'.* The next day Dawn came to the garden to clear her head and decided to keep the secret about Ralph's dismissal. Ralph then came, bowed, and said, *"hi Princess"*. Dawn waved, *"hey Ralph"*. Ralph asks, *"how are you feeling today?"*. Dawn says, *"um...fine.."*. Ralph notices the hesitation in Dawn's voice, and she said, *"I'm actually not allowed to speak to you...."*. Ralph asks, *"who said that?"*. Dawn replies, *"my fiancée, and I have to respect that he is not comfortable with me being with you alone"*. Ralph says, *"fair enough, I can respect that. however, I was sent to search for you"*. Dawn stunned says, *"you were?"*. He nods and replies, *" of course, by your parents."* Mason comes over as Ralph bows saying, *"Prince Mason"*. Mason kisses Dawn's cheek greeting her, *"hello, my sweetheart"*. Dawn says, *"hey Mase"*. Ralph asks, *"Prince Mason, what brings you to this beautiful garden?"*. Mason says, *" let's not make small talk, Ralph. I hate you and I'm curious to know what makes you think I would be ok with you being near my fiancée while I am not around?"*. Ralph says, *"I am her personal guard now"*. Dawn was stunned while Mason wasn't happy. Ralph says, *"I think you may call me her bodyguard or protector. but that's neither here or there, I will be guarding her when you cannot be present until her wedding day."* Mason says, *"I think that is highly unnecessary as I can protect her myself"*. Ralph says, *"I believe the King said that you would need to occasionally return to your country over the next six months- was he wrong?"*. Mason says, *"yes, but I can still protect her"*. Ralph says, *"the King and Queen believe it would be best for me to protect her, I have a lot of skills in marksmanship and also using a sword. I'm somewhat of an expert in both but if you aren't ok with it, Dawn can choose if she would like to have me or you protecting her"*. Mason says, *"fine"*. Ralph says, *"Dawn?"*. Dawn says, *"um... Mason if my parents are saying that Ralph is best suited to protect me, then he is and Ralph has a point that when you aren't around, I need someone to stay by my side. I can't disobey the wishes of the King and Queen. you know that Mason...right?"*. Mason says, *"I am not okay with this, not even a bit. but- I know you are right in not wanting to disobey your parents' wishes. I will be taking my leave since she is apparently in your capable hands, Ralph".* Ralph bows saying, *"of course, Prince Mason".* Mason soon leaves while Ralph says, *"Princess....".* Dawn asks, *"is this really what my parents want?".* Ralph nods replying, *"yes, I promise you".* Dawn smiles and nods while Ralph says, *"I am really grateful that you accepted my protection."* Dawn says, *"you do know I am doing this for my parents, not you, right?".* Ralph says, *"oh, um.. sure".* Dawn says, *"besides, you are an expert marksman and sword fighter, right?".* She rolls her eyes just as Ralph says, *"I thought royalty wasn't allowed to roll their eyes? but I won't tell".* Dawn giggles and thanks Ralph who smiles watching her laugh. Ralph asks, *"Princess, can I speak openly with you?".* Dawn says, *"I guess".* he says, *"Dawn, this may be crossing my boundaries... but I really want you to be happy and if you feel that it is with Mason then I support you. however, I don't want to leave this unsaid; I really do hope that you are happy, but I also must ask... do you have any feelings for me at all? because if so, I want to help you, but if not, I respect that."* Dawn is surprised and replies, *"I am so appreciative of you, and I really love that you are so forward and open with me.*

But I'm with Mason and I do love him. I want your friendship Ralph; I hope that's ok with you". Ralph sadly says, *"I can't say that this was the answer I expected.. but I will support you, no matter what".* Dawn thanks him and asks, *"did my parents actually need me for something though?".* Ralph nods replying, *"yes, they did".* Dawn heads to leave however Ralph stops her asking, *"can I ask you one more question? did you happen to read my letter?".* Dawn nods and heads off while Ralph thinks, *'she doesn't have feelings for me.. she wants to be friends... I should have fought harder for her!... it's too late now..'.* Bethany comes into the garden and sees Ralph who says, *"hey Beth! how are you?".* Bethany replies, *"fine, what about you?".* Ralph tells Bethany about his conversation with Dawn. Ralph says, *"Beth, can I ask you something?"* Bethany nods and Ralph says, *"how has Dawn really been since I left?".* Bethany replies, *"at first I thought she was ok, she started dating Mason the day she got back. her grandma had a way of controlling her, Dawn told me she was upset and mad at you. seemingly you supposedly stole from the kingdom- although I never believed it. but after you were gone, she was really sad and broken. I saw how truly devasted she was. if you want my honest opinion? I think she was going to choose you and what happened broke her heart."* Ralph was surprised and stunned saying, *"do you really think so?".* Beth nods while Ralph asks, *"so there may still be hope?".* Ralph asks, *"how would you like to help me try to win Dawn back?".* Bethany smiles and replies, *"I'm in".*

Chapter 26

Dawn came to see her dad in the throne room. she curtsied and said, *"hi dad"*. Daniel replies, *"hi Princess"*. Dawn says, *"Ralph told me you called for me?"*. Daniel says, *"yes, I did"*. Dawn asks, *"is everything ok?"*. Daniel nods and says, *"I guess I just wanted to discuss your eventual taking over this kingdom, there's going to be a day here where you will take over. of course, hopefully not for a long time."* Dawn laughs and says, *"I hope not!"*. Daniel says, *"I wanted to clarify, there are two ways for you to get the throne. I die, or I give it to you and step down"*. Dawn says, *"I would prefer it not from you dying as I don't know how I'd do right after you die"*. Daniel says, *"I would love to see you take over, how do you feel about it?"*. Dawn replies, *"honestly...don't you think Charlie would be far better at this?"*. Daniel asks, *"why do you say that?"*. Dawn says, *"I know it's my duty as your only child... but I only recently became a part of this world.. am I really the right person to be here? to be running the entire country?"*. Daniel says, *"Dawn, look. no one ever feels good enough to run a country.. I never really thought I was, but I know that I am here for a purpose. I wouldn't have found you if you weren't supposed to run this country."* Dawn asks, *"what about Charlie?"*. Daniel replies, *"what about him?"*. Dawn asks, *"wouldn't he be better to run the country? he has grown up in this lifestyle"*.

Daniel says, *"Dawn, you're right, he has. but you have something that Charlie needs to be the right person to lead this country... empathy... concern... Charlie lacks that and in lacking that- he doesn't know when to place his own selfish desires in front of that of the people. he's proven that, especially lately. He wouldn't be a bad leader. he just isn't the right one"*. Dawn says, *"you think I am, dad?"*. Daniel says, *"very much so, I do. you are an incredible young woman, Dawn. you are going to be a phenomenal Queen some day and you've been training for this. you have to put your own self-doubt to the side and know your worth."* Dawn smiles and says, *" I appreciate that, dad, can I ask you another question?".* Daniel nods while Dawn says, *" I'm getting married here really soon, am I making the right choice to marry Mason?".* Daniel was surprised by her question as she says, *"I really do love Mason, a lot. but I am feeling a little confused right now."* Daniel asks, *"what has you so confused?".* Dawn replies, *"Ralph has.. having him back is making me question myself".* Daniel asks, *"Dawn.. do you still love Ralph?".* Dawn replies, *"what? NO! I love Mason, not Ralph. it's just that I don't think I got to say my goodbyes to Ralph, and it kind of left things opened up. I mean I told Ralph I just want a friendship with him. I just want to know if you as my dad agree with my decision of marrying Mason or not?".*

Daniel says, *"if you are happy and he treats you well, I do. but if you find you aren't happy, you need to express that".* Dawn says, *"but I'm happy".* Daniel says, *"then I am fine with your engagement and soon to be marriage. but can you do me a favour and think about something?".* Dawn nods while Daniel says, *"think about this... are you marrying for love or for your country?. I want to know that this the right thing for you."* Dawn wants to reply however Daniel says, *"I want you to think about it Princess. now, I am going to go spend time with your mother".* Daniel leaves thinking, *'I hope she's marrying for love....'.* Later in her room, Dawn is thinking about her dad's word when Bethany comes in saying, *"hey bestie".* Dawn says, *"hey Beth".* Bethany asks, *" can I discuss something with you?".* Dawn says, *"of course, what's up?".* Bethany says, *"you know I love Daphne right? I mean, I am madly in love with her, and I want to marry her someday."* Dawn was supportive just as Bethany says, *"I have a huge problem, how about the fact that being gay in the royal family is probably a no-no? I don't want to keep hiding us Dawn, I love her."* Dawn asks, *"do you know if she is ready to come forward?".* Bethany says, *"I don't, but I'm really nervous that she will say no. I love her....".* Dawn says, *"Beth, you need to ask her".* Bethany nods and shows a box with a ring. Dawn is surprised while Bethany says, *"we've talked about getting married before. this is actually something I am comfortable in asking her."* Dawn says, *"I understand bestie why you're nervous or sad. I think after five years, she wants the same thing. I think you need to ask her opinion and get this all off your shoulders".* Bethany says, *"if I do, will you be there with me?"* Dawn hugs Bethany and replies, *"of course bestie, I'm always there for you".* Bethany takes a deep breath saying, *"let's do this".* They come to the living room; Daphne has just finished reading a book and sees Bethany and Dawn. Daphne says, *"hey bee, how are you?".* Bethany smiles and replies, *"hey Daph".* Daphne senses a small awkwardness while Dawn says, *"you've got this bestie".* Bethany takes a deep breath saying, *"Daph, we've been together now for a long time. I love you so much and I hate hiding us, I really want us to go public and declare our love openly".* However, before she can say more, just then is a scream, *"AAAAAAAAAAAAAAAAAAAAH!WHAT?!?!??! what the hell did you just say to my sister?".* They all turn to look at Charlie; Bethany says, *"I asked my girlfriend if we could take our relationship public".* Charlie angrily says, *"how dare you? how could you this? both of you? do you know what will happen if this shit gets out?".*

Dawn says, *"hopefully they will be getting accepted by their family, friends and the country they love so much?".* He says, *"how long have you known, Dawn?".* Dawn replies, *"since the holiday trip".* Charlie says, *"it's been that long?".* Daphne says, *"Char, you're scaring me".* Charlie says, *"I should hope so! you need to learn where your place is little sis!".* Bethany says, *"can we please not argue about this?".* Dawn says, *"look, Charlie. I get this is a huge shock to you. when I found out it was to me too. but can't you be happy for your sister? she's found true love!".* Charlie angrily , *"I will never ever be happy about this thing they have going on! NEVER!".* Daphne comes in front of her brother and says calmly, *"Char, please-".* Charlie furiously says, *"don't you ever call me Char again! you are not my sister! you are a freak and abomination; the King and Queen will be informed of this".* He slaps her leaving the others shocked. He leaves while Daphne cries and Bethany says, *"how dare he raise his hand on* you! *Daph, baby are you ok?"*. Daphne cries and says, *"no, he hates me! he hates me so much!"*. Bethany hugs Daphne and says, *"baby, he's just in shock"*. Dawn says, *"I agree but that doesn't excuse that fact that he just slapped her"*. Daphne says, *"I never thought he would hurt me like this"*. Bethany says, *"I promise you Daph, he will never hurt you again"*. Daphne worries about telling the King and Queen however Dawn says, *"I believe my mom will support your relationship and I think my dad will be very understanding, welcoming and supportive too"*. Daphne says, *"I hope so"*. Dawn says, *"let's go and speak with them"*.

Chapter 27

Dawn brings the girls to the garden for some fresh air. Ralph comes and bows saying, *"hello Princess Dawn, Duchess Daphne and Bethany"*. Ralph says, *"you have been summoned by the King and Queen immediately"*. Dawn says, *"thanks, Ralph"*. Daphne and Bethany head in while Dawn says, *"I'll see you later, Ralph"*. Ralph stops her asking, *"Dawn can I ask for a moment of your time?"*. Dawn nods and replies, *"yes, but please let me go be with Daphne and Bethany, they need me. how about I meet you near the pond where we usually meet?"*. Ralph says, *"ok Dawn, I'll be waiting"*. She leaves while Ralph thinks, *'I hope she will turn up'*. Dawn comes in and apologises for being late. Daniel says, *"we were just about to speak with your cousin and friend here about some shocking news we received"*. Bethany says, *"please don't believe what you heard.. I'm sure it has been twisted or fabricated"*. Daniel says, *"I want to hear your version of what's going on"*. Daphne says, *"uncle, please don't judge us. it just happened, overtime I fell madly in love with Beth. I can't bear your rejection and if you do, I will leave with her. I just love her so much I could never live without her."* Daniel says, *"after hearing everything Daphne, I have only one thing to say... I am so incredibly happy that you have found someone who makes you this happy."* Daphne was in shock as was Bethany; Dawn says, *"I knew my parents would support you"*. Amelia says, *"Daniel and I see Bethany as an adopted daughter, this is your home and if you are two together we happily support that"*.

Daphne and Bethany thank Daniel and Amelia and hug them happily. Daphne says, *"Charlie isn't happy"*. Bethany says, *"being gay is just something we didn't think the crown or royal family would be so accepting of"*. Daniel says, *"times are changing though, we are required to be more accepting of each other in order to be a more peaceful world. someday girls, you will have to tell the public if you intend to take this further but for now, enjoy being together and we will cross that bridge when we come to it".* Daphne hugs Daniel and says, *"thank you once again, uncle".* Daphne and Bethany leave however just before Dawn can go; Amelia calls her back; Daniel and Amelia both says, *"have a good night, sweetie".* Dawn leaves while Amelia asks, *"Daniel? are we going to tell her?".* Daniel replies, *"yes my love, soon because she has lot going on right now".* Amelia nods as she says, *"I hope she's happy...".* Daniel kisses his wife replying, *"she will be ok".* Amelia ask, *"are you happy hubby?".* Daniel replies, *"beyond happy, wifey. I think it's time to head to bed".* Elsewhere, Ralph was by the pond waiting when Dawn comes and yawns. She says, *"hey Ralph".* Ralph says, *"you came, Dawn".* Dawn rolls her eyes and giggles, *"of course, I said I would".* He asks, *"are you ok?".*

Dawn nods and replies, *"yeah, just tired".* Dawn says, *"do you mind if we do not talk?".* Ralph says, *"whatever you wish, Princess".* They soon look up at the sky which is shining bright with thousands of stars. Dawn thought, *'his presence is so calming... he's so peaceful and kind... being by Ralph's side... I just love having him beside me.. I missed him... more than anything in the world... time hadn't aged him at all... he was still handsome and sexy... oh no!'.* Dawn then breaks down while Ralph hugs her in his arms and still thinking, *'I don't know why I let this hug happen, maybe it's because I needed it without knowing it... maybe it's because his touch and comfort was all I needed.. I do love Mason... but Ralph has always been by side from the moment I found out I was a Princess... he's been kind, protective, friendly and everything I ever wanted... he's always supported me in my journey... I felt so many emotions.... anger for Ralph leaving... happy for Daphne and Bethany'.* Ralph asks, *"Dawn, are you alright?".* Dawn replies, *"yeah, thank you for your presence".* Ralph asks, *"do you want to talk about it?".* Dawn tells Ralph everything and feels a huge weight off her shoulder. Ralph says, *"you do know that I am here for you no matter what, right? you've always been someone I've admired.. I think I always will... you are incredible.. you're gorgeous, fun, lively and there's nothing I wouldn't change about you. I think you will be an amazing Queen someday. I am not happy you want to be with Mason. I won't lie to you on that. but I support your love for him, and I still love you, Dawn. I won't ruin your relationship; I just want you to know that another reason your parents wanted me to protect you when he's not here".* Dawn says, *"me too, ralph".* Mason soon came over and says, *"is everything ok here?".* Dawn smiles and replies, *"yes, it's fine thanks".* Ralph nods too. Mason says, *"Dawn, your father needs you".* Dawn was confused however Ralph says, *"I will let you two speak in private, goodnight".* Mason says, *"really, Dawn?".* Dawn says, *"excuse me?".* Mason says, *"I keep telling you not to be alone with him and I always find you alone with him!".*

Dawn says firmly, *"excuse me, Ralph is a dear friend of mine, and I will not have you disrespecting him or my parents. My parents have said he is to be my bodyguard and therefore, he is guarding me".* Mason apologises and says, *"I just don't like him being around you. you and him had a past at some point... I don't want old feelings coming up.. I love you Dawn".* Dawn says, *"you're lucky, I love you too. but you can't get annoyed at me for this".* Mason asks, *"how did you both end up here?".* Dawn replies, *"I went for a walk, and he happened to be here, I really didn't want to speak to him or anyone. I just needed peace and quiet".* Mason comes over and kisses her however Dawn says, *"it's getting late, I'll see you tomorrow".* Later that evening, Mason and Charlie meet at the bar. Mason says, *"so many drinks, so little time".* Charlie says, *"you should learn how to hold your alcohol better".* Mason laughs saying, *"you should learn to loosen up, Charlie-boy!".* Mason had another few shots and felt drunk. Ralph came in and said, *"I need a drink".* He saw Charlie and Mason getting drunk and wondered, *'what are they doing here? I don't want a fight... I'm keeping my distance'.* Mason says, *"I can't believe that he's back, after all this time, he's back".* Charlie says, *"too bad, he's back."* Ralph thinks, *'I am sure they are talking about me....'.* Mason says, *"I am thinking of asking Dawn to come back with me; I don't know if she would go for it, but I want to try".* Charlie says, *"even if you persuade her, good luck convincing uncle. she's his only child and he adores her".* Mason says, *"hey, I can try. you know what?".* Charlie says, *"what?".* Mason says, *"I can't believe the King and Queen let that piece of shit back into the castle".* Charlie says, *"I guess you are talking about Ralph".* Mason nods while Charlie says, *"honestly, I'm not surprised at all. he sees Ralph as the son he never had".* Mason says, *"well I wish he would leave, secretly disappear forever, I hate his smug ass".* Charlie says, *"you only hate him because he almost took Dawn from you".* Mason says, *"but I sent him away, so of course, I won".* Charlie says, *"I guess so".* Ralph angrily thought, *'so it was your fault, you bastard! I'm going to record this.'*

Chapter 28

Mason says, *"I wish I could have seen his face when Queen Matilda fired him."* Charlie says, *"I am not at all interested in him, he's not the first guy I've gotten fired from the castle for nothing and he won't be the last".* Mason laughs saying, *"you're terrible dude!".* Charlie says, *"you're also drunk off your ass!".* Mason laughs and says, *"I am glad you let me be part of taking his ass down! what made him think he would have had a chance with royalty?".* Charlie says, *"he's dreaming above his pay grade, so there's that".* Mason says, *"I wish the help would just get it through their heads to just let us royals be".* Ralph stops filming and thinks, *'I guess that's enough. I have evidence that they were behind my dismissal, so I think I'm good now'.* He watches as two ladies approach Charlie and Mason. Charlie says, *"hello, ladies".* The girl in red hair says, *"hey boys".* Mason says, *"hello sexy dolls".* They giggle while the girl in blond hair asks, *"how are you boys tonight?".* Charlie says, *"much better now that you are here."* The girl in red hair asks, *"have you had enough to drink yet?".* Charlie says, *"I think my buddy here has had enough for the both of us".* Mason says drunk, *"I could have more if I wanted too..".* Charlie says, *"Allyssa, my love would you like to accompany to a room?".* Allyssa says, *"sure, hunk".* Charlie says, *"I would very much like to experience something new tonight, if you know what I mean".* He playfully winks and they both head off. Ralph thinks, *'disgusting animals'.*

The red hair says, *"so, Mason?".* Mason says, *"hey sexy".* Mason asks, *"how do you know Charlie?".* Lily replies, *"Charlie and me are playmates if you know what I mean".* Mason asks, *"do you think we can be play mates tonight?".* Lily says, *"sure, sexy".* Mason feels tired and asks, *"do you know any good motels around here? I need to sleep off this buzz".* Lily giggles and says, *"buzz? I think there's a good one nearby".* Mason says, *"let's go".* Lily says, *"am I invited?".* Mason nods while Ralph thinks, *'what the fuck? If I follow them, I can record this too... I hope he doesn't do anything that could hurt Dawn. I need to keep an eye on this.'* Soon in the motel, Mason flirts with Lily and says, *"I hope you don't mind spending the night with me baby doll".* Lily says, *"I'm sure I won't mind it at all."* Ralph witnesses this from outside and thinks, *'I need Dawn to see this, she's going to be heartbroken, but she deserves better than this scum...'.* Back inside, Mason removes his clothes and says, *"mmmm Lily keep kissing me... ohh yes.. I like it like that... fuck you're sexy...".* Back outside, Ralph finishes filming and think, *'I can't believe him... he's a lying, disgusting piece of shit! I can't believe he would hurt Dawn like this... poor Dawn... I have to go show this to the King.. I hope Dawn can forgive me for this'.*

The next morning, Charlie and Mason were waiting in the throne room. Mason says, *"I wonder what they want from us this morning".* Charlie says, *"whatever it is should have been able to wait".* Mason says, *"my hangover is the worst".* Charlie says, *"I told you to quit drinking".* Mason says, *"whatever".* Daniel, Amelia, and Ralph come in. Daniel says, *"good morning, gentlemen".* They both bow and greet Daniel who says, *"I wanted to ask you both where were you last night?".* Charlie says, *"we went out for a few drinks last night, we got a little too drunk and slept at a local motel, uncle".* Daniel asks, *"Mason, do you agree with Charlie?".* Mason nods while Daniel asks, *"what were their names?".* Mason asks confused, *"excuse me? I'm not sure what you mean".* Daniel says, *"I think you both do. I have pictures and videos".* Mason was shocked asking, *"what? how?!".* Charlie says, *"you're terrible at hiding things".* Ralph shows the footage from his phone while Mason asks, *"how the hell did you get these?".* Ralph replies, *"you were out in public, and I happened to spot you in the bar boasting".* Daniel angrily says, *"you are in far more trouble than either of you could imagine! care to explain?".* Charlie says, *"so what? all turned out as it should; Dawn is in love with Mason, and it doesn't matter what happened to Ralph. he's nothing more than a servant, a help... and besides, Dawn is doing the right thing in returning the bloodline to something more purely royal".* Daniel angrily says, *"HOW DARE YOU DISRESPECT YOUR QUEEN LIKE THAT!"*. Charlie replies, *"she's not my queen!"*. He yells, *"LEAVE! I WILL DEAL WITH YOU LATER!"*. Charlie heads out while Mason says, *"I apologise on his behalf"*. Daniel says, *"you need to be worried about yourself now, not him."* Daniel says, *"Amy my love, please give us some space"*. Amelia was stunned however Daniel says, *"I promise you, we will talk later, ok? you need to rest, please"*. Amelia leaves while Ralph asks, *"is the Queen ok?"*. Daniel replies, *"she's fine, just very tired lately"*. Daniel turns back to Mason and says, *"you, young man are NOT permitted to marry my daughter- EVER! I will never allow her to marry such scum as yourself!"*. Dawn comes in and says, *"excuse me, dad? why can't I marry my fiancée?"*. Daniel says, *"Princess, hold on."* He turns to Mason saying, *"are you going to tell her or should I?"*. Mason says, *"I am so sorry, Dawn."* Dawn says, *"sorry? sorry for what?"*. Mason says, *"I was responsible for Ralph's removal from the castle."* Dawn was shocked while Daniel says, *"what else?"*. Mason says, *"I can't do this"*. Daniel angrily says, *"TELL HER NOW OR I WILL!"*. Dawn says, *"Mase?"*. Mason sighs and replies, *"I slept with someone last night"*. Dawn felt angry and said, *"how could you do this to me? how could you disrespect me like this?"*. Mason says, *"Your Highness, Ralph, can I please speak to Dawn alone?"*. Daniel nods and says, *"yes, but then I expect you to leave my kingdom"*. Mason bows and says, *"of course, sire"*. Daniel says, *"I am sorry, Dawn"*.

Daniel leaves while Ralph asks, *"do you want me to stay?"*. Dawn says, *"it's fine I've got this"*. Ralph says, *"ok, I'll be waiting outside for you when you're ready"*. Dawn asks, *"Mason would you care to explain what happened?"*. Mason says, *"it was an accident"*. Dawn angrily says, *"it was an accident that you went with her to the motel, got naked, and had spent the night with her"*. Mason says, *"I'm really sorry, Dawn"*. Dawn asks, *"tell me, how many times has this happened?"*. Mason says, *"um... it's been quite a few times but not just with Lily"*. Dawn says, *"I can't believe you Mason! this was a big concern of mine with dating you! you crossed the line here! why, Mason? why?"*. Mason replies, *"because, Dawn, I have needs too. sex is important to me, and I had to-".* Dawn says, *"so because I wouldn't sleep with you, you cheated on me?! I told you from the start I was waiting until marriage! I can't believe you! we are done Mason. take your shit and leave!".* Mason says, *"please think again, I love you Dawn".* Dawn rolls her eyes and says, *"you clearly don't! now leave before I get the guards to throw your ass out!".* Mason soon leaves and Ralph comes back inside. He asks, *"Dawn, are you ok?".* She replies, *"I need space, Ralph".* Ralph asks, *"would you like me to walk with you in the garden?".* Dawn says, *"I need to be alone, please".* Ralph says, *"I am here if you need me."* Dawn begins to cry and runs out while Ralph thinks, *'I want to go after her, but she says she needs space, and I must respect that.'*

Chapter 29

D aniel comes in asking, *"where's Dawn?"*. Ralph replies, *"she ran out crying and said she needed space, sire"*. Daniel says, *"it might be the best solution right now, she needs to clear her head and if she's anything like her mom, she will be highly emotional right now"*. Ralph asks, *"is the Queen ok? emotional?"*. Daniel says, *"you'll know sooner or later... we just found out a few weeks ago, but... the Queen is pregnant"*. Ralph was surprised, congratulated Daniel, and asked, *"does Dawn know about this?"*. Daniel replies, *"no, not yet. but we will tell her soon"*. Ralph asks, *"are you excited?"*. Daniel says, *"more than I can explain. I've always wanted a family, now I have my daughter, my wife, and a new child to add to it I couldn't be happier."* Ralph asks, *"so what is going to happen to Mason and Charlie?"*. Daniel says, *"honestly, I am going to banish them both. Mason needs to leave to give Dawn space and time to heal and trust again. Charlie on the other hand is trash; if he can't respect the current Queen and future Queen, he can leave"*. Ralph says, *"what's going to happen to Dawn now?"*. Daniel says, *"who knows? it's her choice in the end what happens?"*. Ralph nods and says, *"if you don't mind now Ralph, I have a former nephew of mine to teach a lesson too"*. Three months pass, Dawn kept herself locked up in her room, distancing herself from her friend.

Dawn soon came out into the garden and looked at the flowers blossoming. She thought, *'I needed to sort things out... it was a shock finding out I would no longer be marrying the man I thought was my love... he destroyed me.. my heart and head ached more than anyone can ever imagine... in these three months... I needed my heart to heal'.* Ralph comes into the garden and sees Dawn in deep thoughts... He bows and says, *"I apologise, Princess. I didn't know you were here, outside"*. Ralph says, *"I will let you get back to your thoughts"*. Dawn says, *"wait,*

Ralph". Ralph says, *"yes, Princess?"*. Dawn says, *"it's Dawn to you and not Princess"*. He nods and smiles while she asks, *"do you mind staying here with me?"*. Ralph says, *"of course, um... how are you feeling?"*. Dawn says, *"I'm ok.. better than I thought I would be at this point atleast"*. Ralph says, *"that's an improvement then"*. Dawn smiles and asks, *"can you let me know what I've missed?"*. Ralph asks, *"have your parents not told you?"*. Dawn says, *"nope, they are busy on the new baby and managing the kingdom. I can't believe at 21 I am going to be an older sister"*. Ralph says, *"well, Daphne and Bethany made their relationship public which is a good thing considering they are engaged to be married."* Dawn says, *"I feel so bad, that I haven't been there for them these past three months"*. Ralph says, *"they miss you, but they understand and gave you space"*. Dawn says, *"what else?"*. Ralph says, *"well, I'm sure you are aware that Charlie has been banished from the kingdom as well as Mason."* Dawn smiles and says, *"I am, I believe it was for the best too. and you Ralph? how have you been?"*. Ralph says, *"I'm fine, actually. I've been missing you a lot though; I've been worried about you. everyone has..."*.

Dawn says, *"I've changed a lot"*. Ralph asks, *"in what way?"*. Dawn says, *"I guess growing up a lot and becoming more aware. I don't trust people not in the same way I used to"*. Ralph sadly says, *"I am sorry to hear that Dawn"*. Dawn asks, *"do you know why?"*. Ralph asks, *"why, what?"* Dawn says, *"why Mason cheated on me?"*. Ralph shaked his head as Dawn replied, *"I wouldn't sleep with him"*. Ralph says stunned, *"you didn't sleep with him?"*. Dawn giggles and says, *"I guess this is new in this time, but- I wanted to save myself for my husband and for marriage. I'm still a virgin"*. Ralph says, *"well, I think it's disgusting that he would cheat on you because of that. any man who cheats over not having sex in a relationship is trash. If he didn't respect your wishes enough to just be a good man- that's his loss. you need someone who will always love and respect you."* Dawn thanks Ralph who says, *"Dawn, can I tell you something?"*. She says, *"sure, Ralph what is it? I'm always here to listen"*. He says, *" ok, well, thing is... I love you extremely Dawn. ever since I laid my eyes on you from the first moment we met. you are extraordinary, beautiful, smart, funny and to me.. perfect. I would kill to just see you smile every single day. I want to be the one who makes you smile. I want to be the one you come to when you have a bad day or problem. the one you fall asleep next to for the rest of time. the one who will always love you unconditionally. I want to be the one who teaches you to trust again... I want to be your 'Prince'. I love you Dawn, I always have, and I always will."* Dawn cries happily while Ralph says, *"I didn't mean to make you cry, Dawn..."* She says, *"it's ok, Ralph. I'm crying happy tears because you make me so happy. I have strong feelings for you Ralph, but I'm scared. I don't want to feel heartbroken or be hurt again".* Ralph says, *"Dawn, I promise you, I will never hurt you".*

Dawn felt emotional for a moment while Ralph says, *"if I tell you a secret, do you promise not to judge?."* Dawn nods while Ralph says, *"I've been waiting until marriage myself. I just wanted my first time to be with my wife".* Dawn was stunned and asked, *"you're a virgin too?".* He nods and replies nervously, *"yeah....".* Dawn says, *"that's incredible, Ralph... I mean, I wouldn't judge you if you had either- but I'm kind of glad to hear you value that. it's something I respect myself".* Ralph says, *"I respect your choice too."* Ralph says, *"Dawn? I just have to ask you... will you atleast give me a chance to prove myself to you?".* Dawn hesitated however Ralph says, *"I have an idea to prove my love for you".* He pulls her close, dips her and kisses her passionately. Dawn thought, *'it feels like fireworks! I could feel his passion, his love, his desire, all in this kiss. I felt home, safe, and comforted... for the first time in three months, I felt at peace. it all made sense to me finally'.* Ralph brings her back up asking, *"are you ok, Dawn?".* She smiles and says, *"I am".* He says, *"I really do love you, Dawn".* She says , *"I know".* Ralph says, *"I hope you consider giving me a chance".* She says, *"I am considering it."* Ralph asks, *"how can I persuade you make a decision?".* Dawn says, *"another kiss might help".* They kiss passionately until someone interrupts them.

Chapter 30

Bethany says, *"I totally approve of this"*. Dawn says, *"oh, hey Beth"*. Bethany says, *"three months of silence and I walk into this scene. don't you dare tell me bestie that you were hiding this from me all this time!"*. Dawn laughs saying, *"no way!"*. Ralph says, *"it just kind of happened"*. Bethany says, *"good, because I love and ship it!"*. Ralph says, *"I should let you two catch up. I will see you later, Dawn"*. Dawn blushes and replies, *"absolutely Ralph"*. Bethany says, *"Dawn you are glowing"*. Dawn thanks her while Bethany asks, *"are you sure you're ok with this?"*. Dawn nods saying, *"I couldn't be happier and more confident than I am right now in this decision"*. Dawn says, *"sorry, I haven't been around lately"*. Bethany understand and says, *"you had a lot going on, no worries."* Dawn says, *"I heard a rumour that you and Daphne are engaged"*. Bethany shows the ring and says, *"we are"*. Dawn says, *"I can't wait to see you both get married to each other!"*. Bethany says, *"I must have my bestie at my side as my maid of honour"*. Dawn says excitedly, *"seriously?"*. Bethany asks, *"did you really think you would be a bridesmaid?"*.

Dawn says, *"I guess I just never thought about it."* Bethany says, *"I love you bestie, and I'm glad you're back"*. Dawn hugs Bethany saying, *"I am, and better than ever before"*. Seven months pass; Dawn has been very busy learning about more royal responsibilities. Amelia comes in with her son in her arm. Daniel asks, *"how's my little Kayden?"*. Dawn says, *"I will let you have a moment dad"*. Daniel says, *"hold on Dawn"*. Daniel gives Kayden to Dawn to hold. He coos happily in her arms. Dawn says, *"I love you so much little bro"*. Dawn looks at the time and says, *"dad, I have a date with Ralph tonight"*. Dawn gives Kayden back to Amelia and heads off to her room. She calls Daphne and Bethany to help her get dressed. Dawn thinks, *'I am so happy that me and Ralph found our way back to each other... over the last few months we started our relationship slowly however... things began to get deeper... hotter and heavier I mean....* Later that evening, Dawn came out into the garden to find a picnic laid out for her. She sees a note and picks it up... she read, *"you are my light, the one shining in the starry night sky, the sun burning me and who's absence would plunge me in the dark...it didn't start with a kiss but with a glance.. our love is like a never-ending story...".* Dawn looks around and suddenly looks back to see Ralph on his knee holding a box saying, *"Dawn my love, I can't imagine a life without you... will you marry me?".* Dawn has tears in her eyes and nods. Ralph puts the finger on her hand and lifts her kissing her passionately in his arms. Dawn says, *"I love you Ralph".* Ralph says, *"I love you more, Princess".* A few weeks later; Dawn goes wedding dress shopping. Bethany says, *"will you hurry up, Dawn?".*

Daphne says, *"babe, you need to calm down".* Bethany says, *"this is wedding dress shopping! my bestie's getting married! TO RALPH!!!".* Bethany does a dance while Daphne says, *"I'm so happy for her, it's about time she joined the club".* Bethany says, *"you're silly, babe but I love you".* They share a kiss just as Dawn comes out and tries several different options. Dawn eventually choose a simple yet elegance white pearl lacey dress. A few days later; it's finally the wedding day, Dawn is in her room almost ready as she looks in the mirror and takes a deep breath; the door opens and Amelia says, *"I can't believe my little girl is all grown up".* Dawn says, *"mom, you're going to make me cry".* Amelia says, *"I have something for you".* Amelia gives her a silver bracelet which has engraved, *'the best is yet to come'.* Dawn wears it and hugs her mom while crying happy tears. Dawn wipes them and leaves with Amelia to meets her dad downstairs. Daniel says, *"ready, Princess?".* Dawn nods and Daniel walks her down the aisle; she sees Ralph looking at her with tears in his eyes. She comes over to Ralph who says, *"you look so beautiful Princess".* The priest says, *"we are gathered here to unite...".* Ralph says, *"Sorry priest, we have our vows ready, can I please?".* Ralph says, *"Dawn, ever since the moment we first met, I fell in love with you.*

you are amazing in every way... you're kind, cute, funny and someone I want to forever hold in my arms, I want you to be the first person I see when I wake up and the last person to cuddle at night.." Dawn says, "*Ralph, every day I find myself falling in love with you more, you believed in me when I thought I couldn't do it; you are not just my soulmate but my best friend too*". The priest says, "*do you Raphael take Dawn as your wedded wife?*". Raphael says, "*I, Raphael, take you Dawn to my wife. I promise to be true to you in good times and in bad, in sickness and in health. I will love you and honour you all the days of my life.*" The priest says, "*do you Dawn take Raphael as your wedded husband?*". She replies, "*I, Dawn take you, Raphael, to be my husband. I promise to be true to you in good times and in bad, in sickness and in health. I will love you and honour you all the days of my life.*" They exchange the rings as the priest says, "*I now pronounce you husband and wife, you may kiss the bride*".

They share a passionate kiss as everyone showers confetti and rose petals on the happy couple. Ralph lifts Dawn in his arm who thinks, '*this wedding was so amazing... our family and closest friends... I couldn't have asked for anything more perfect'.* Later that evening, Dawn and Ralph were kissing each other passionately. Ralph stops asking, "*are you ok wifey?*". Dawn replies, "*I am a little nervous, hubby*". Ralph says, "*me too.*" Dawn says, "*I do have a little surprise for you though*". She heads into the bathroom while Ralph takes a deep breath and comes out of his suit. She soon comes out wearing a red nightie. Ralph is stunned and speechless while Dawn asks nervously, "*um- do you like it?*". Ralph says, "*you look sexy, Princess*". They share a kiss, and each say, "*I love you*". Ralph carries her to the bed and lays her down. She wraps her arms around him and pulls him closer. Dawn says, "*take me to the heaven tonight*". He says, "*as you wish my Princess*". Elsewhere in another kingdom, Charlie brought a newspaper filled with pictures of Dawn and Ralph's wedding. Mason came out into the living room and said, "*I can't keep this up*". Charlie says, "*it's your own fault*". Mason says, "*you're not in a much better place*". Charlie says, "*I am actually, I married into royalty, and you didn't".* Mason says, *"it's not like I had a choice".* Charlie says, *"you shouldn't have got Lily pregnant".* Mason says, *"I wish I'd never been with her".* Charlie says, *"too late now".* One year passed happily since the marriage of Ralph and Dawn. Daphne, Dawn, and Bethany were hanging out in the living room watching a movie; Bethany and Daphne were more interested in kissing and making out. Dawn didn't know why but she felt tired and got up quietly and came into her room however before she could sleep, Bethany and Daphne came in saying, *"where did you disappear to like that?".*

Dawn says, *"you both were busy, I didn't want to disturb you".* Dawn yawns while Bethany asks, *"you've been feeling very tired lately haven't you?".* Dawn nods while Daphne asks, *"do you think she could be?".* Bethany says, *"maybe...".* Dawn says, *"what are you both whispering about?".* Bethany asks, *"is there a possibility you could be pregnant?".* Dawn laughs replying, *"no, I'm not nauseous or anything".* Bethany says, *"I think you are".* Dawn yawns and says, *"fine, I will take a test after my nap".* They leave the room while Dawn heads to the bathroom and takes the test; she soon heads to bed. A few hours later, Ralph comes and sees Dawn sleeping. He heads to the bathroom and screams, *"OH MY GOD!!".* Dawn wakes up and comes to see Ralph by the pregnancy test. He asks, *"Dawn, what's this?".* Dawn replies, *"it's a pregnancy test".* He asks, *"so... why isn't it negative?".* Dawn sees the plus line and starts to panic however Ralph says, *"would you mind taking another test, it could be a false positive?".* Dawn does the test again and calls Ralph back inside; she cries says, *"it's positive!".* Ralph is shocked however he lifts Dawn into his arm and kisses her passionately. Ralph says, *"I'm going to be dad!".* Dawn says, *"you want to be a dad?".* Ralph nods replying, *"only since, forever. are you pleased about it?".* Dawn says, *"it's still a shock".* Ralph hugs Dawn saying, *"I love you Dawn, and I am here for you and our baby. I can't wait to be part of every step of this journey".* Dawn says, *"I love you too Ralph".* Soon, they broke the news to their family and friends who were over the moon. Three years later, Dawn was in the garden watching her kids play; Ralph came over with a tray of lemonade and cookies. Ralph says, *"how is our fourth bundle of joy?"*. Dawn giggles and says, *"I can't believe we are here... I miss mom and dad though..."* Ralph says, *"they will be back soon"*. Ralph and Dawn share a kiss as their daughter Charlotte says, *"mommy, I want to have a sister next"*. The two boys come over and take the lemonade and cookies. Ralph says, *"I will check on the boys"*. Charlotte sits by her mother's side while Dawn cuddles Charlotte saying, *"I am sure, I will be able to bring you a little sister"*. Charlotte says, *"I love you so much mommy"*. Dawn kisses her daughter's cheek and says, *"I love you too Charlotte"*. Just then two boys come over and see a last cup of lemonade and begin to fight. Daphne says, *"stop fighting you two"*. Dawn smiles seeing Bethany and Daphne coming and they share a hug. Ralph watches the kids while Dawn says, *"I don't know how we managed to get here"*. Bethany says, *"it's been a rollercoaster ride"*. Dawn laughs as she sees Ralph playing with the kids when suddenly she feels a pain in her stomach. She screams, *"RALPH!"*. Daphne says, *"oh no! she's about to give birth"*. Bethany says, *"I will watch the kids!"*. Ralph carries Dawn to the car, and they drive to the hospital. After several hours of labour, Dawn gives birth to her second daughter. Ralph says, *"she's so beautiful"*. Bethany asks, *"have you thought of a name for her?"*. Dawn says, *"Juliette"*. Ralph holds his daughter when soon the kids come in followed by Amelia and Daniel. Dawn thinks, *'it's been a long journey, but I wouldn't change a thing because from finding out that I was born to royalty to having the most amazing incredible husband in the world... truly I wouldn't change a thing'.*

CPSIA information can be obtained
at www.ICGtesting.com
Printed in the USA
LVHW080325260522
719743LV00011B/423

9 798201 938086